"I'm going to get to my truck and take the gun out of the back. Do you want to wait inside it?"

She flashed him a wry smile. "What do you think?"

"I think you want to come with me, but I also think you'd better consider what's good for Charlie. He needs his mom."

"Point taken," she conceded. They ran to the truck, and Lily slid inside while Chance took his revolver out of the locked case and handed her the keys. "If anything goes wrong, get yourself out of here, okay, Lily?"

"Chance, I—"

"Not now, sweetheart," he said. "I'm in a hurry. Lock the doors. I'll be back." He leaned inside and kissed her. Her lips were cool and wet and perfectly delicious. He tore himself away and ran toward the back of the church.

COWBOY UNDERCOVER

Alice Sharpe

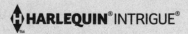

I'd like to dedicate this book to all readers
who, just like me, love a good story.

Recycling programs
for this product may
not exist in your area.

ISBN-13: 978-0-373-69877-6

Cowboy Undercover

Copyright © 2015 by Alice Sharpe

Printed in U.S.A.

Alice Sharpe met her husband-to-be on a cold, foggy beach in Northern California. Their union has survived the rearing of two children, a handful of earthquakes, numerous cats and a few special dogs, the latest of which is a yellow Lab named Annie Rose. Alice and her husband now live in a small rural town in Oregon, where she devotes the majority of her time to pursuing her second love, writing. You can write to her c/o Harlequin Books, 233 Broadway, Suite 1001, New York, NY 10279. An SASE for reply is appreciated.

Books by Alice Sharpe

Harlequin Intrigue

The Brothers of Hastings Ridge Ranch

Cowboy Incognito
Cowboy Undercover

The Rescuers

Shattered
Stranded

The Legacy

Undercover Memories
Montana Refuge
Soldier's Redemption

Open Sky Ranch

Westin's Wyoming
Westin's Legacy
Westin Family Ties

Visit the Author Profile page at Harlequin.com for more titles.

CAST OF CHARACTERS

Chance Hastings—This former ladies' man has met his match in Lily Kirk. He knows she's the wrong woman for him and figures if he helps her out of her current mess, it will get her out of his system for good.

Lily Kirk—After years of an abusive marriage, she ran away with her small son. Then she fled her sanctuary, the Hastings Ridge Ranch, after a botched attempt on her life. Now her son is missing, and she turns to the one man she's trying to forget for help.

Charlie Kirk—Lily's little boy's middle-of-the-night call for help instantly galvanizes Chance. Who can say no to a frightened five-year-old?

Jeremy Block—Lily's estranged husband is a powerful district attorney with secrets. Will those secrets destroy him and everyone else around him?

Wallace Connor—Killed months before by a man who turned himself in for the crime. Wallace's murder seems cut-and-dried, but is it?

Darke Fallon—Wallace's self-acclaimed killer, he seems to be at the center of everything.

Tabitha Stevens—This teenager was Wallace Connor's younger girlfriend. By all accounts she took his murder hard. Will she be the killer's next victim?

Robert Brighton—His father started White Cliff, a survivalist community in the Idaho panhandle, decades before. Robert presides over White Cliff now, but even he has forgotten everything there is to know about the place, which could be a costly oversight.

Elizabeth Brighton—Robert's wife is an enigma. Sick in body and soul, she's lost contact with some very important concepts. What will her husband do to protect her?

Maria Eastern—Elizabeth's sister has relocated to White Cliff with her two teenage sons. She certainly seems to have her finger on the pulse of the place. Chance is pretty darn sure she knows more than she's telling.

Chapter One

Chance Hastings couldn't sleep. This in itself wasn't un-usual, not lately anyway. Between the extra ranch work an early fall demanded, his brother Frankie's antics and his own personal chaos, his mind was just wound up too tight. What was unusual was that instead of being in his own cabin two miles over the ridge, he'd elected to spend the night at the main ranch house in the home in which he'd been raised. His father and his new stepmother, Grace, had taken a short trip to Oregon and Chance had volunteered to watch over the house as Frankie was rarely around anymore.

Finally admitting there was no point lying in bed with his eyes wide open, he got up and dressed by the light of the full harvest moon shining through the gen-erous window. He'd always loved autumn in Idaho, es-pecially around the ranching community of Falls Bluff. The golden fields rising to the mountains and the decid-uous trees bleeding yellow, orange and red into the high evergreen forest engaged him at every turn.

His plan for the coming day included traveling out to-ward the mountains with his brothers Pike and Gerard to round up the heifers they wanted to move closer to the ranch for the coming winter. He might as well get a head start on things by saddling up three horses and loading them into the trailer. He paused in the kitchen to start a pot of coffee and leave his brothers a note about meeting him in the barn. He pinned the note to the corkboard by the door.

The perking coffee created a warm ambience in the kitchen that he rarely experienced anymore. Lily, who had shown up under mysterious circumstances nine months earlier and left after a sudden fright six months after that, still dominated the room, at least for him. He could almost picture her at the stove, an enigma of a woman who had wormed her way under his skin. He waited for the coffee to perk, but the more aromatic it became the less he wanted it. Instead, he headed for the mudroom where he retrieved his Stetson from the shelf on which he'd stashed it hours before, grabbed his coat and snagged his truck keys from the hook. As he clasped the doorknob and twisted, the phone back in the kitchen rang. His first instinct was to ignore it. He didn't really live here. However, calls in the middle of the night always telegraphed urgency.

"Hello?" he said as he grabbed the receiver.

He heard breathing but nothing else.

"Hello?" he repeated.

A child's voice said tentatively, "Is Mommy there?"

Was this someone's idea of a joke? "Who is this?" he demanded.

"Charlie."

Lily's five-year-old boy? At three thirty in the morning? "Charlie, this is Chance Hastings. Where are you? Where's your mom?"

"I don't know," the child wailed.

"Calm down, big guy. Are you lost?"

"I want Mommy."

Chance's brow furled as his imagination suggested all sorts of reasons for the child to have lost track of his mother. None of them were good. "Charlie? Your mom and you don't live here anymore, remember? You guys left. Do you know where you went?"

Soft sobs filled Chance's ear. "That's okay," he crooned. He could picture the boy's blond hair and blue eyes, freckles scattered over tearstained cheeks. "I'm trying to help you. When did you see Mommy last?"

"Yesterday," Charlie managed to choke out.

"Then what happened?"

"I went to school on the big bus."

"That's great. What's the name of your school?"

"Miss Potter's kindergarten."

Chance doubted that was the actual name of a school. "Do you know where it is?"

"On the little hill."

"Do you remember the name of the hill?"

"No."

"Do you remember the name of the town you and your mom live in or maybe which state it is?"

"I forget. I want my mommy."

"Okay, we're working on it. What happened at school yesterday?"

"I made a picture."

This was like pulling teeth. "Charlie, who are you with now?"

"Daddy."

The phone in the kitchen was the old-fashioned rotary type. Chance's grip on the receiver tightened. He didn't know much about Charlie's father, Jeremy Block, except that he'd done something severe enough in Lily's eyes that she'd run from him with their child in tow and hid out here until Block sent someone to abduct and kill her a few months before so he could reclaim his son. The man had been adamant he was working for Jeremy Block.

The night that went down, Lily left Hastings Ridge Ranch, Charlie in tow. Chance didn't know where Block lived and he didn't know what had happened in the weeks following Lily's departure.

He hadn't wanted to know. He'd avoided the topic like the plague. "Where is your dad right now?"

"Asleep."

"Has he hurt you?"

"No."

"Okay, that's good. Can you tell me anything about where he lives?"

"In a house."

"What city?"

"Bossy."

"Could it be Boise?"

"I guess."

Another thought jumped to the foreground of Chance's mind. Lily would never willingly let her son go unless she had no choice and that meant almost anything from abduction to murder.

"When did you go with your dad, Charlie?"

"Mommy wasn't at the bus stop," Charlie said, talking fast now, his voice wavering as he apparently turned his head and compromised the signal on a cell phone. "A man said he knew where she was. He drove the wrong way and I was scared. I told him to stop but he frowned at me. I fell asleep and it got dark and then we were at Daddy's house but I want Mommy and he says I can't see her and—"

"Charlie!" A masculine voice boomed from Charlie's end of the line. "What are you doing, boy? Is that my phone? Who did you call?"

"I want Mommy," Charlie squeaked.

The man spoke into the phone. "Lily? Do you really think you're ever going to see him again?"

"This isn't Lily," Chance said.

"Then who—"

"I'm a friend of Charlie's. Are you Jeremy Block?"

"What's it to you?"

"The boy sounds upset. What's going on?"

"Nothing that concerns you," Block said, and severed the connection.

The ranch phone didn't have a caller identification screen so Chance dialed the code to find out the number of the last call, jotted it down and dialed it. The call was answered by Block's terse message to leave a number but now Chance knew that Charlie was in Boise or a nearby community with the same area code.

Chance called a Hastings family friend on the police force next, Detective Robert Hendricks, who had a knack for sounding alert and on the job no matter when you yanked him from slumber. Chance told him about the call. "Give me the number," Hendricks said.

"You've got to rescue the boy," Chance said.

Hendricks was quiet for a beat or two. "Gerard told me you didn't want to know anything about Lily Kirk after she left the ranch. Was your brother mistaken?"

"No. I didn't want to know anything. I still don't. But it's different now that Charlie is in jeopardy."

"Charlie isn't in jeopardy," Hendricks said slowly.

Chance straightened his shoulders. "What? How can

you say that? Are you forgetting Jodie Brown and what he did to Kinsey thinking she was Lily?"

"Stop for a minute, Chance. Jeremy Block is a respected district attorney in Ada County down in Boise. Lily ran out on him and took their child with her. She has a documented history of being unstable. He filed for and won temporary custody in her absence. It sounds as if he finally got his kid back. As a father, I can understand how good that must feel. The fact is Lily is the loose cannon, not him."

"But Jodie—"

"Jodie Brown was a career criminal with a record as long as your arm. Block sent him to prison for drug trafficking twelve years ago. He says that's the last time he saw him. He figures Jodie was out to take revenge on him by abducting his wife and demanding a ransom. Block denies having anything to do with Jodie since years before when he won the conviction. There is no indication he isn't telling the truth."

"What does Jodie Brown say about this?"

"He's dead. His truck ran into a tree a couple of days after he left your ranch. His blood alcohol was .20. Case closed. Except that there's a warrant out on Lily but I understand she's disappeared."

"If Jeremy Block knew where to find his son, he knows where to find his ex-wife," Chance said, and despite Hendricks's insistence that Jeremy Block was Man of the Year material, felt a chill.

"Not ex," Hendricks said. "There's been no divorce."

Chance blinked away that momentary shock. "Charlie said a man took him from the bus stop and drove him to his father's house. Doesn't that remind you of what Jodie

Brown tried to do? Do you really believe Jeremy Block is telling the truth?"

"I really do," Hendricks cautioned. "But more importantly, it's all happening two hundred miles from here. The police in Boise are satisfied with his story so that's the end of it although I will contact them about the child's call so they can look into it."

Chance slammed down the receiver. His father had taken Lily in nine months earlier and not said a word to anyone about her past but there was a good chance he knew something that might help. Chance had to know she was safe and not fighting for her life somewhere. He dialed his father's cell and when no one answered, his stepmother's. Both phones went straight to voice mail and he left the same message, an insistent request they call home as soon as possible.

Now what? Where was Lily? How did he find her?

He heard a vehicle outside. Undoubtedly Gerard or Pike had arrived early to help get ready for the Bywater trip. He dashed into the mudroom, glad for the company. He was betting Gerard knew all about Lily's past from Hendricks. He switched on the floodlights before opening the door and exited the house as a woman stepped out of a red coupe.

The car looked familiar but the small woman standing in the glaring light did not. The three resident dogs had roused themselves from their beds in the horse barn to welcome the newcomer who didn't seem alarmed by the excited attention of the two shepherds and the part-Labrador retriever milling around her legs. She wore her light brown hair parted in the middle and pulled back. Heavy black glasses dominated a pale face while a long shapeless gray cardigan dominated an equally drab dress that fell all the way to the top of brown cowboy boots.

"Chance?" the woman cried, taking a halting step forward and then stopping.

Chance's mouth almost dropped open as he recognized Lily's voice. For the tick of a heartbeat he tried to reconcile the woman before him with the sassy, blonde firecracker who had left here months before, and then he came out of his stupor and stepped toward her. "I just had a call from Charlie," he said.

"You heard from my baby? When?" Her hands flew up to cover her face and her knees buckled. He reached her before she hit the ground. The dogs yipped with uncertainty.

"I'm okay," she insisted. "Where is Charlie? Who has him?"

"His father," Chance said.

"I thought so. Damn."

He still couldn't believe she was here and right on the heels of the past thirty minutes of revelations. He was touching her, almost holding her. He'd only done that once before and at that time, he hadn't known she was still married. And at that time, at least at first, she'd melted into him…

"Come inside," he said. "I just made coffee."

"I need to talk to your father."

"Come inside," he repeated. "You're trembling."

"How did Charlie sound?" she asked as she allowed him to guide her up the stairs.

"Not bad," Chance said because he couldn't bear to tell her how frightened the boy had seemed. "I don't know why he called here looking for you."

"It's my fault. I drilled this number into his head last summer when my cell phone died."

The dogs hung back at the door. Chance led Lily to a stool and she sank down with a shuddering sigh. He found mugs and poured coffee. "I contacted the local police and asked a detective friend for help."

"The police?" She took off the thick glasses and closed her eyes, squeezing the bridge of her nose with thumb and forefinger. "I wish you hadn't done that," she said, looking back at him. Without the glasses, her rich brown eyes came into focus and she looked more the way he remembered her.

"Yeah, I can understand why you'd rather not have to discuss your husband with the cops," he said. "Did you know there's a warrant for your arrest?"

"It doesn't surprise me. It's probably the first thing Jeremy did when he realized I wasn't coming back."

"What's it for?"

"I'd lay my money on kidnapping my own child."

"Because of your troubled past?"

She narrowed her eyes and he saw a flash of the old Lily. "I don't have a troubled past. That's Jeremy's story, not mine. Where's your dad?"

"He's gone. He won't be back for a few days. Tell me why you stole off into the night with Charlie. Not the time you did it three months ago when you left here. Before that, when you left Jeremy."

She shook her head as she undoubtedly picked up the anger his words hadn't been too successful at disguising. "You don't need to know."

"Listen, Lily. Jerk me around all you want but in the end, who else is going to help you? Dad is off in Oregon. There's a good chance he's out of signal range. Unless you have legions of friends I don't know about, maybe we should just level with each other."

"Don't start this, Chance. You and I can't agree on anything. There's no point in involving you—"

"Involving me?" he snapped. "You come here in the middle of the night dressed like you're auditioning for the role of the prim librarian in *It's a Wonderful Life*. Your son, the best thing you've ever done as far as I can see, has been taken by his psycho father and you're so frightened your eyes are spinning. Trust me, I'm involved."

"I don't want you—"

"I know. You made that real clear last summer. I'm not asking you to sleep with me, I'm asking you to let me help Charlie. Now, what do you say?"

She rubbed her forehead and he wondered how long she'd been driving. Where had she gone after she left the ranch? He waited for her to make up her mind, and when it seemed they would sit there in silence forever, he decided to wade in. "Block told the police Jodie Brown was acting on his own to take revenge on him for convicting him twelve years ago. By the way, Jodie died in a traffic accident before the police could question him. The case is closed as far as they're concerned.

"Furthermore, Block is claiming you had a history of being unstable and that you took your son without giving him a chance to work something out with you."

"He didn't want a chance to work things out," she said. "You don't understand—"

"Of course I don't," Chance said. "You haven't given me the opportunity to understand because you haven't said anything. Start with something easy. How was Charlie snatched?"

Her fingers tightened on her mug as she leaned forward. "I had a flat tire yesterday so I was running late to meet him at the bus stop. Everything just seemed to go wrong and it got later and later. I called the school but the bus had already left so I called one of the other mothers and she said she would pick him up when she got her own child. I went to her house but Charlie wasn't there. She said she'd arrived a minute late and seen him getting into a car with a man but he was smiling so she figured I sent another friend. She described him. It sounded enough like Jeremy—I could guess what was happening."

"But it wasn't Jeremy. Charlie told me a man he didn't know told him he'd take him to see you but he drove to Boise instead."

"Poor Charlie," she cried. "He must have been frantic. Why didn't I have a better plan for days like that one? Why did I live so far away from his school that he had to ride a bus? He hates buses. I should have found a different job closer to his school—"

"Calm down," Chance said, patting her hand. "Is he in any danger from his father?"

She stared at him for a second. The look in her eyes twisted his heart but he ignored it. Then she finally shook her head. "Not immediate danger, no. Jeremy is in love with the idea of having a son, making a legacy, although the reality of it bores him. He can be violent, but mainly toward me. Near the end the violence was trickling down to Charlie. He's not suitable to raise a child."

"I guess that's what he says about you, too," Chance observed.

"I know. He's twenty years older than I am. When you're adrift and all of nineteen, that kind of attention from a man like him is pretty exciting. He could do anything, or so I thought. He raced cars, he rode horses, he flew a plane—anything. Long story short, I wound up pregnant. He insisted we get married and I thought I'd hit the jackpot. At first I barely noticed the way he didn't want me associating with my friends or holding down a job. I just thought he wanted to take care of me. My father was an alcoholic. It was…nice…to have a man take charge for a change."

"But eventually?"

"After Charlie was born, Jeremy started taking on high-profile cases to make a name for himself. It wasn't enough to just be a prosecutor anymore. He wanted me as arm candy at parties to impress the 'right' people. I hated those parties and he knew it. In fact, I suspect he knew my heart wasn't in our marriage anymore. At some of those parties, I felt so light-headed and disconnected I was afraid I was going to pass out. People looked at me funny and made comments I wasn't supposed to hear about how I was a drunk like my father. The thing was, I didn't drink anything but seltzer. Jeremy told me it was my nerves and for a while I kind of believed that. I was so blasted stupid I made things easy for him.

"Then one day I found a bottle of barbiturates in Jeremy's desk drawer and I knew in a flash that he'd been drugging me so I'd appear intoxicated in front of other people. I worked up the courage to ask for a divorce. He said I was welcome to leave as long as I left alone. I protested, of course. I planned to take Charlie, but Jeremy promised that would never happen. He said everyone knew how paranoid I'd become, and that I drank. He said I'd trapped him by getting pregnant and everyone knew that, too, and felt bad for him. He said it would be better all the way around if I just died. That way he would get total control of Charlie and be a sympathetic widower to boot. He laughed when he said it, but you have to know Jeremy. His laugh has nothing to do with humor."

"So you bolted," Chance said. With her now austere hair and colorless clothes, she actually looked like the kind of person life beat into submission. He suddenly missed her bleached hair and dangling earrings and then it occurred to him that perhaps that persona had been as much a facade as this one.

"More or less," she said. "I started gathering every scrap of paper I could find, every receipt, anything that looked potentially valuable. I found a few photographs, made copies of records… Anyway, they're all in a safety-deposit box in Boise. I've never tried to make sense of them, there was never time. I just knew I needed something on him if I was ever going to win custody of Charlie. I was hoping I'd find evidence of collusion or something. But then he came home one night and he had had a horrible day. He'd been riding high after winning a conviction against a child murderer and his name was being discussed in political circles. But then a kid hanged himself in his cell and the prosecutor's office came under investigation. Jeremy was livid.

"Anyway, I didn't say the right thing or look the right way, who knows? Jeremy hit me so hard I blacked out and when I came to, Charlie was sitting beside me, crying. I'll never forget the look on his face. A week later, I'd made my plans and Charlie and I left. The mother of an old school friend took me in for a day or two and then she called your father and he offered me a job and refuge so that's how I ended up here."

"You never called the police?"

"No. I'd tried that before and wound up looking like a nutcase trying to ruin my husband's reputation. It wouldn't have done any good. Jeremy was respected, and feared, by so many people and I was a nobody."

They both startled and got to their feet as engine noise came from the yard.

"I hope that's not the police," Lily said. By now they were at the back door and could see through the small window.

"It's Gerard's truck," Chance said. "We're going up to get the heifers today." He opened the door and watched his brother approach. Gerard had had a couple of rough years, starting with the tragic accident that had taken the lives of his wife and daughter, followed by a spell of amnesia. But he'd come out on top when he fell in love with Kinsey Frost, the woman who helped him find himself in both a literal and figurative way.

Gerard stopped walking as Lily stepped out onto the porch beside Chance. He tipped his hat and said hello the way a cowboy does to a female stranger.

"It's me," Lily said, moving down the steps to intercept him.

He still looked confused.

"Lily," she added, coming to a stop in front of him. Gerard looked from her to Chance. Chance knew that his older brother and Kinsey were probably the only two people in the world who understood what it had meant to him when Lily left and he crossed mental fingers now that Gerard wouldn't spill it. He should have known he wouldn't. Gerard gave her a hug and then looked around. "Is Charlie asleep in your car?"

"He's not with me," Lily said.

"Come inside," Chance added. Lily turned to come back up the steps. In a moment of clarity, he saw the terror lurking in back of her eyes.

"Kinsey is going to be so sorry she missed seeing you," Gerard added as they once again closed the doors on the three dogs. "She flew back to New Orleans to help her grandmother for a couple of days. How long are you going to be here?"

"I'm leaving in a few minutes," Lily said. "I wanted to ask your father for advice. I thought maybe… Oh, I shouldn't have come."

"We can give advice, too," Gerard said as they entered the house.

"A lot is going on," she said, picking up the glasses she'd taken off when she first arrived. She folded them into a pocket and added, "Chance can fill you in after I've left."

"No, Chance can't," Chance said but he suspected Gerard didn't need too much filling in.

"Why?" Lily demanded.

"Because I'm coming with you."

"You don't even know where I'm going," she protested.

"You're going to Boise. You're going to see Jeremy Block. You'll need someone to bail you out of jail."

A defiant expression crept onto her face. "You don't have to do that," she said, thrusting her chin high in the way the Lily he'd known before used to. That woman he had chided and baited and given a rough time and she had returned it all with a spirit that intrigued him to this day. "I don't need someone to take care of me," she added.

"Yeah, right. Anyway, we'll stop at my place so I can throw some clothes into a duffel, tuck a big fat gun under the front seat and then we're off."

"What is it about men?" she asked no one in particular. "You all think you can rescue the damsel in distress."

"Well, when the damsel shows up so early in the morning, what are we supposed to do?"

"Listen when she says no thanks."

Silence ensued until Gerard cleared his throat. "May I say something?"

"Sure," Lily said.

"Just take him along for the ride, will you please? He's impossible when he gets like this and he might actually come in handy."

She looked at Chance, who silently returned her scrutiny. She was beautiful under all that drabness, delicate and feminine as long as she didn't start arguing. But he couldn't wrap his head around the thought of her leaving on this mission all by herself. If she refused to let him come with her, he'd follow on her tail.

"Oh, all right," she said.

"Unless Frankie shows up, you and Pike will have to get the heifers on your own," Chance told his brother.

"We'll manage," Gerard said as he poured himself a cup of coffee and added with a wink, "You two kids be careful."

Chapter Two

"Explain one thing to me," Chance said.

Lily had been staring out the dark passenger window, her eyes gritty from fatigue. She'd asked Chance to take the wheel because she'd been driving for hours and knew her judgment was impaired. She turned her attention to Chance whose strong profile was undeniably spectacular, a fact she found irritating. She didn't want to like him or need him or want him around and the fact that she felt all those things to some degree just plain irked her. "What do you want to know?"

"Last summer when Block sent Jodie Brown to take you, he had murder on his mind. If he had a warrant and had established custody of Charlie, why didn't he just turn you in? Why all the drama and hysterics? Why take such a risk?"

She shrugged. "How am I supposed to know that? All I can figure is that he doesn't want to share custody with me. Maybe Jeremy has the police in his pocket but if we end up in court, twelve ordinary people will get to hear my side of things. That might bring out distasteful facts about his true character. Plus, he's no doubt looking ahead to his future campaign for governor. That's his goal, you know. I could pose a liability to him."

For a second she heard her father's voice in her head. In a moment of sporadic sobriety he'd warned her not to look back, to keep focused on the future. *You can't change the past*, he'd said, and he was right.

But you couldn't run from it either and that's exactly what she'd done.

"Does Block know about those papers you gathered?"

"Probably. I raided his file drawer that last day. Maybe he's afraid I have something on him. Wouldn't it be wonderful if I actually did? I need to get them out of my safe-deposit box and take a look."

"Before you see Block?"

"I have to have some kind of ammunition."

Lily closed her eyes, hoping to find a few minutes' respite, but Chance had other ideas. "If he had murder on his mind before, why did he take Charlie this time and leave you free to continue causing trouble?"

Weariness had long ago seeped into every cell of her body. Talking was a struggle. She cradled her forehead with her hand. "I don't think that was his plan," she said. "Remember I told you about all the mishaps that made me late? I think he was not only making sure he could nab Charlie but that I would arrive home alone. But I didn't go home. I called a neighbor who promised to call immediately if Charlie showed up. For hours I just drove around and then I thought of your father."

"One more question," Chance said.

"Please, I'm exhausted."

"I know you are, Lily." He put his hand on her arm and even through the sweater, his touch made a warm spot that spread toward her shoulder.

"One more," she agreed.

"Where did you go when you left the ranch?"

"Reno. I figured hiding on a remote ranch hadn't worked, so I decided to try a bigger city. I drove to Reno because I had a friend there who said she was leaving town for a few weeks to visit her boyfriend in Florida. She said I could use her apartment and sub at her old job as a waitress at one of the casinos outside of town. Now I'm wondering if my friend ran low on funds and told Jeremy where I was to collect a little quick cash."

"She's like that?"

"She could be. For all I know Jeremy set the whole thing up with her just to nail down my location. I don't know. I try not to be paranoid."

"With a warrant out for your arrest, you probably shouldn't have taken Charlie over a state line."

"I didn't know about the warrant," she said. "You just told me about it. It wouldn't have made any difference though." She turned in the seat. "I think that's how Jeremy found me this summer. He must have accessed Idaho school records. My decision to send Charlie to summer school could have gotten me killed."

They fell silent. She leaned to the side until her forehead rested against the passenger window and closed her eyes. For a few moments she waited for Chance to think of something else he wanted explained, and then she stopped worrying about it. The next thing she knew, Chance was shaking her shoulder.

"We're here," he said as she rubbed the sleep from her eyes. "What now?"

They were in Boise, downtown somewhere. She'd been gone for almost a year but she'd lived here most of her life. She finally recognized the café on the corner and placed their exact location. "My credit union is a few blocks that way," she said, pointing north. "I want to get that stuff out of my safe-deposit box."

Chance glanced at the clock on the dashboard. "It won't be open yet. Let's grab something to eat."

"Not in this district," she said. "Jeremy's office is pretty close to here."

"Just give me directions."

Despite commuter traffic, they were soon approaching the suburbs and a plethora of fast-food establishments. Settling on one, Chance ordered himself a full breakfast but she stuck to coffee, knowing her nervous stomach wouldn't take kindly to food.

What was Charlie doing right that moment? Had Jeremy employed someone to help him take care of him? Was Charlie afraid he'd never see his mom again? The poor little kid had a fragile spirit that she'd no doubt fostered by putting up with Jeremy's abuse for so long. She wanted him to be braver about life than she'd been.

Chance plowed his way through half the menu, proving what Lily knew from months of cooking on the ranch: Cowboys could eat. As he was wadding up wrappers and tossing them into the bag, he met her gaze. "You should have something besides coffee," he said.

"Maybe later. Is it still too early for the credit union to be open?"

He turned the keys and the clock flashed on. "Yeah. Let's stay right here in the back of this dark little parking lot until it's time."

"I guess," she said. What else were they going to do?

"Great." He smothered a yawn with his fist as he pushed the lever to half recline the seat. "I'm going to catch forty winks. You okay?"

Did he mean beyond the gnawing nerves and the constant worry? "I'm fine," she said.

With a little smile, he tipped his dark brown Stetson down over his face, crossed his arms over his chest and seemed to go to sleep in about thirty seconds flat.

For a while, she stared at the comings and goings in the parking lot. Who knew so many people bought their breakfast at a drive-through? That made her think of Charlie who loved fast food and her eyes burned. She wanted to be on the move, not stuck here waiting.

She looked over at Chance when he made a soft little sound as his hand slipped from his chest. She caught it before it landed on the gearshift, carefully returning it to rest beside his other hand.

In a way she wanted to remove his hat and gaze at his sleeping face. Without the cynical glint in his dark eyes that often caused her to look away, would she glimpse the man she'd felt pull at her heartstrings so many months before?

She allowed herself to remember the night last April when they'd been walking alongside the river. Wildflowers had perfumed the air and the still-cold water gurgling against the rocks sounded like music. They'd stopped beside a tree and she'd leaned against it and before she knew it, he had cupped her face with both of his hands and told her she looked beautiful in the moonlight. His gentle voice and soothing caresses had been a balm to her broken spirit so that when he finally kissed her, she was flooded with feelings she'd given up hope of ever experiencing.

Eventually, he'd unbuttoned her blouse and lowered his head to kiss her throat, his lips warm against her cool skin. She'd wanted him with every fiber in her body, yearning for the moment when he stripped her bare. That moment never came because she'd been yanked back to reality when the plaintive call of a coyote rose from the ridge. The terrible decisions she'd made concerning men and desire all seemed to storm through her head as the lonely cry echoed over the valley. She'd withdrawn emotionally and he hadn't been so far gone that it escaped him. With a sigh, he'd raised his head and looked down into her eyes and she'd bolted, running back to the ranch house like a scared rabbit.

Their budding romance had died that night and eventually turned into an acerbic interchange of half-veiled insults and sarcasm.

Yet here they were.

"Knock it off," she scolded herself. "Think of something pleasant."

"LILY? LILY, WAKE UP," Chance said for the second time that day, he shook Lily's shoulder.

She was slow to respond at first and then she sat bolt upright. "Oh, God, I fell asleep. What time is it?"

"Almost one. We slept for hours."

She rubbed her forehead. "Well, at least the credit union will be open. Let's go."

Once inside the building, Chance looked askance at all the security cameras and wondered if anyone there knew about the warrant out for Lily. Thanks to the black glasses and baggy clothes, she looked more like a refugee from a homeless camp than a patron of a downtown banking establishment, but would someone call the cops as soon as she announced her identity? He decided to keep his fears to himself and just stay alert for any sign of trouble.

She went through the security measures to access her

box and disappeared with the attendant. A few minutes later, she returned, a couple of fat manila envelopes peeking from the top of her oversize handbag. He took her arm and they left together. The whole thing had taken less than fifteen minutes.

"We need to find someplace private to go through and sort all this," she said as she hugged her purse as if it was a precious baby. "I'd forgotten how much stuff I collected."

"Let's get a room somewhere," Chance said.

"Good idea."

They found a room and paid using Chance's credit card and name. Once inside, Lily removed the thick glasses before upending both envelopes onto the small round table. The contents came spilling out.

"Yikes," Chance said. The thought of trying to make sense of all that paper was mind-boggling. Maybe he should have stayed at Hastings Ridge and rounded up heifers, which was a lot more fun than pushing papers around. Of course he didn't say any of this to Lily who would just remind him he was here because he'd wanted to be.

She flashed him an understanding smile and sat down. "I think we should get the clippings into one pile, receipts into another, memos into a third and miscellaneous off over there."

For more than an hour they sorted and organized in near silence. Chance was anxious to do something about Charlie and he knew Lily was, too. It made sense to try to find something she could use against Block in some way, but it seemed unlikely they had sufficient time to make such a discovery.

"Let's go to your husband's house," Chance finally said. One more useless receipt and he was going to scream.

"No. He doesn't get home from work until six thirty or so."

"So we'll get there before he's home."

"Not a good idea. I want to catch him unaware."

"You said earlier that he knew you'd come after Charlie."

"I know, but he doesn't know when or how. Be patient."

"We're not going to be able to wade through all of this in one afternoon," Chance said, gesturing at all the bits and scraps of papers before them.

"You're probably right. I'm going to go take a shower and change clothes. I hope the clothes in my emergency escape suitcase still fit."

Chance walked over to the window. He stood looking out into the parking lot for a few minutes. Was she getting gussied up for Jeremy Block? That was a disquieting thought.

With a sigh, he returned to the papers. Thirty minutes later, his heartbeat quickened as he detected the first clear pattern he'd come across in the form of several orders from a florist shop in Boise. He stacked them apart in order of ascending dates. The deliveries were spaced at intervals of seven days and all went to the same address. Without knowing his way around this city, he had no idea if they went to an individual or a business. For all he knew, they could be flowers Block purchased for his office or his secretary's desk or even for the house he'd shared with Lily.

For a second he rubbed his eyes. The long nap in the car had taken the edge off fatigue, but he was still tired. Sleep had been so elusive lately. He felt if he laid his head down he'd fall into slumber for a hundred years and wake up ready to punch Block in the nose, reunite Charlie with his mother and take them both back to the ranch and…

Wait a second. Was this about Lily and the fantasy he entertained on long nights that someday he and she…

Oh, please, don't go that route, he cautioned himself. *Don't pretend because she needs your help she actually wants you.*

He looked up when a noise at the bathroom door caught his attention. Lily emerged with her soft brown hair waving around her heart-shaped face. Gone were the baggy dress and long, limp sweater, and in their place, tight black jeans, a black form-fitting top and a brown leather belt that matched her boots. She'd gone from plain Jane to a country-Western knockout and he swallowed a jolt of desire that shot through his body like a lightning bolt.

"Feel better?" he managed to say in a voice that sounded remarkably steady.

"A lot better," she murmured. Her gaze dropped to the stack in front of him. "Did you find anything?"

He tore his mind from the lovely curves and dips of her body around which the top had molded itself. "I don't know. Where is Vance Street?"

"Vance. I'm not sure."

He punched the address into his phone and showed her the resulting map. "That's over in the Tower District," she said. "Mostly condos."

"But you and Jeremy didn't live there?"

"No. His family had money of its own. When his father died, he left Jeremy a house and a little land right outside the city. Jeremy pictures himself lord of the manor."

"He sent flowers to this address once a week for several months near the end of the period when you lived together."

"Flowers? Really?" she said as her huge brown eyes came alive. "Jeremy hates cut flowers. I don't think he ever bought me a single rose. There must be a special reason why he did that."

"It could be nothing," Chance cautioned.

"Or it could be he was seeing someone else," Lily said. "Oh, my gosh, I bet he was having an affair. This is great!" She started pacing the room again, gesturing, suddenly animated. "If he's involved with someone else, maybe I can use that as leverage." She grabbed her handbag off the back of a chair and the baggy gray sweater from the bed. "Let's go check out that address."

He took the keys from his pocket, ready for action of any kind.

1801 VANCE STREET turned out to be located within a small villa of condos arranged around a central courtyard, all encased within the confines of an ornate iron fence. At this time of year, the pool had been drained and covered in preparation for cold weather. The trees were a riot of color, leaves drifting to the ground as the wind teased them loose.

They found a row of brass mailboxes built into a small arch near the street. The name on 1801 was V. Richards.

"Vicky, Valerie, Vivian?" Lily mused.

"Or Vincent, Victor, Val," Chance said.

"How do we find out?"

"We ask."

She looked around at the complete absence of other people and raised her eyebrows.

"Look, at the risk of making you mad, how about you let me knock on the door and see what I can find out."

"Why you?" she said. "I'll do it."

"What if this person is actually home and what if you know them or they recognize your face? You aren't disguised, remember?"

"I know. But so what?"

"So they call Block, Block calls the cops, Charlie spends the next twelve years living with daddy dearest."

"Oh."

"Just go sit in the car, okay?" he coaxed.

"Okay, but don't mess this up."

"Your faith in me is truly heartwarming," he said. "Here, take my hat with you so I don't stand out so much." He waited until she got back in the car, then he walked down the narrow path to 1801. He wasn't surprised when no one responded to the doorbell as it was a late weekday afternoon. He imagined the tenant of the condo was still on his or her commute. He walked around the grounds looking for someone, anyone, and finally spied a middle-aged guy raking leaves out by the pool/patio area.

"Excuse me," he called. "I have a delivery out in the truck for 1801, V. Richards. They're not home. Is there a manager here or anything?"

"I'm the manager," the man said, leaning on his rake. He gave Chance a once-over, probably deciding he didn't look much like a delivery man but glad for anything that interrupted the raking, especially as the fading light must make the job a tough one. "What can I do for you?"

"Is it safe to leave a package outside the door? It's pretty heavy. I wouldn't want it to be a problem for the recipient to get it inside by themselves."

"Yeah, it's safe enough. That door doesn't face the

street. If Valentine needs help, all she has to do is ask for it. She's a nice enough kid."

"Kid?"

He laughed. "Everyone under thirty is a kid to me and she's way under. Probably nineteen or so."

"Does she live alone?" Chance asked and immediately wished he hadn't. But the manager didn't seem to find the question intrusive.

"Oh, you mean how does a gal her age afford this place? Easy. She's a student. Her parents pay the bills and they wanted her someplace safe."

"So she lives off her folks and goes to college," Chance said, hoping he sounded like a jealous guy who had had to support himself his whole life and begrudged Valentine her address on easy street.

"Yeah, tough, right? She's been here for two years now. Well, kids these days, you know." His gaze suddenly focused over Chance's shoulder and he straightened up. "Hey there, Mr. Hasbro."

Chance turned to see a grumpy-looking man in his late sixties. "The circuit breaker blew again. You need to fix it pronto."

"Sure thing, Mr. Hasbro. As soon as I finish raking…"

"No, now. Betty is in the middle of making my dinner."

"I'll be right up, sir. Just have to get my tools."

"Don't dawdle," the older man said and stalked off.

"His breaker wouldn't blow if his wife didn't overload it," the manager confided to Chance. "Just leave the package," he added as he set aside the rake and hurried off.

"Well?" Lily asked as he slid into the passenger seat.

"You were right, it's a woman, but I don't know. The manager said she is a nineteen-year-old student."

"She sounds perfect," Lily said. "Jeremy likes his women young and innocent."

"Her name is Valentine Richards," Chance added. "The manager seems to think she's a nice kid."

"That's all he said?"

"Pretty much."

"It's going to have to be enough," Lily said.

"Enough for what?"

"Leverage. You don't send a woman flowers for weeks on end without there being a motive."

"Maybe, but Lily, even if he was having an affair, you left him. Unless this woman is a convicted criminal, he's just an abandoned husband with a girlfriend."

"But it appears he was seeing her while we were married."

He shrugged. "Today's morality doesn't necessarily blink at infidelity."

"It's all I've got," she added. "Are you coming with me or not?"

"Let's get it over with," he said as he felt around under the seat with his right hand, reassured when his fingers brushed the smooth leather of the holster into which he'd slid his .38 over twelve hours earlier when they'd stopped at his cabin.

SHE KNEW HER way around the city, taking backstreets, avoiding long-winded lights, anxious now to get this over with.

"You can't just walk into his house and have a simple conversation with him, you know," Chance said.

She flashed him a quick look. He'd all but disappeared in his dark clothes in the dark car. Just the glint of the whites of his eyes and the occasional street lamp illuminating his face. "That's exactly what I'm going to do," she said. "I'm going to tell him I know about his affair with Valentine. That's my leverage."

"He'll chew you up and spit you at the police department."

"Doesn't matter. It's a chance I have to take. Maybe he'll listen to reason."

"Maybe he'll listen to Smith and Wesson," Chance said, and took the gun from under the seat. The thought of the two of them eye-to-eye with a gun in the middle made her anxiety level shoot through the roof.

She pulled the car over to the side of the road, parking between street lamps where darkness prevailed.

"We're here?" Chance said, looking around.

"No. The house is a block over. I didn't want anyone to recognize my car. Come on."

They walked quickly. She knew a shortcut that consisted of a nature trail owned by the home owners' association and took him that way. They erupted onto the street she'd called home for five years. The thought of stepping foot on Jeremy's property made her physically ill. The only worse scenario was losing Charlie. She would not leave here until she'd at least seen him. "I'm going to try reason," she muttered to herself as they drew closer.

Chance sighed. "Nothing you've said about this guy screams reason, Lily. Listen, let me go in first," he added. He shoved the gun into the back of his jeans. "I'll be reasonable. He won't know who I am so he won't be expecting anything. I can at least make sure Charlie is in the house and—"

"No," she said softly but with fire in her tone, pulling on his arm to stop him from proceeding. "The house is right up there. Someone could be guarding the gate. You stay back here so he doesn't see you."

"Have you forgotten what your husband did to you, Lily? Are you crazy?"

"He's not going to risk killing me in his own home."

"You are crazy. You've told me what he did to you in his own home."

"I was a lot more timid back then. And I didn't have Valentine Richards to use as ammunition. Please, Chance, just wait for me. Like you said on the ranch, I might need someone to bail me out of jail."

With that, she continued walking, relieved beyond belief when Chance didn't follow. She didn't look back until she reached the gate. There was no sign of Chance.

"Evening," a man said.

She turned to face the gate. She'd never seen the man standing there.

"May I help you?" he asked.

"Who are you?"

"Name's McCord," he said. "Who are you?"

"I'm Jeremy's Block's estranged wife. I need to talk to him."

McCord's face registered surprise as thick eyebrows wrinkled his brow. He was a stocky, fifty-year-old guy with an ex-boxer's nose and a smoker's gravely voice. "I reckon he'll be surprised to see you." He rolled open the gate for her and she followed him up the walkway to the big black door.

"Mr. Block is probably in the study," McCord said as he gestured for her to enter the house. Stepping inside felt like entering a time warp.

"Is anyone else in the house?"

"Besides me? Just the gal Mr. Block hired to watch the kid."

"Then Charlie is here," she said, her gaze flying up the stairs. She veered that direction but McCord stepped in front of her.

"He's here. But you came to see his father, right?"

"After I say good-night to my boy," she said.

"No can do," McCord said and started to reach for her arm to prevent her from climbing the stairs. She dodged his grasp, walked to the study and yanked open the door.

Jeremy glanced up from his seat behind his desk. He was on the phone.

"Wait outside," he barked, his gaze traveling from Lily to McCord. "I'm in the middle of something important." He turned in his swivel chair so that his back was toward them. McCord grabbed Lily's arm and pulled her out of the room. He closed the door and pointed at a chair set against the wall.

Could she get past him and run up the stairs? Charlie was up there, so close now she could almost feel him in her arms.

"Don't try it," McCord said, accurately reading her body language."

"Please, Mr. McCord. Charlie is my child."

"I don't want to hurt you," McCord said and firmly pushed her down onto a chair. He planted himself square in front of her. "But that doesn't mean I won't."

Chapter Three

For twenty-one minutes, according to the clock in the foyer, Jeremy kept them waiting. Lily had no choice but to accept the fact she wasn't getting past McCord, but that didn't keep her gaze from repeatedly traveling to the second floor and the open balcony railing that surrounded it. She was so nervous and stressed her hands trembled in her lap and she had to clench them together to keep herself from exploding. More than once, she caught McCord casting her a distasteful glance.

What exactly had he been told about her?

At last Jeremy's voice told them to come into his study.

"You can leave," he told McCord as they entered. McCord turned and left, closing the door behind him.

Looking straight at Lily, Jeremy trotted out what she called his campaign smile. "Well, look who came home," he said. He did not get to his feet. His sandy-colored hair showed a few gray streaks, his eyes were so blue she knew he wore contact lenses to boost the color. He was dressed for the office in a custom-made gray suit. It was one of the more expensive worsted wools, which probably meant he had been in court that day.

Was he handsome? Not in the way Chance was, not with classic features, broad shoulders and a devilish smile that ignited the color of his eyes. But he was commanding. His cold eyes could look warm when he put in the effort and he knew how to twist words more adroitly than a clown manipulating balloons into giraffes.

She stepped to the far side of his desk. "First of all, this is not my home. Secondly, of course I came. You stole my son."

"The law sees it the other way around." He nodded at his phone. "I should warn you. The police will come as soon as I ask them to. They have a warrant—"

"I know about that." She'd had twenty-one minutes to cool her heels and face reality and what she'd decided was that she was going to have to do the whole thing the legal way and that meant going through the system. "Listen, Jeremy," she pleaded. "Just let me see Charlie. I have to know he's okay."

Jeremy chuckled. "How very melodramatic. Of course he's okay. He's back where he belongs and no longer at the mercy of his unpredictable mother."

Lily's chin tilted. "You might be able to fool other people, Jeremy, but you can't fool me. I'm the one who lived here. I'm the one you set up to look like a lush. I'm the one you knocked unconscious. And then there's that minion you sent to kill me, Jodie Brown."

"You're delusional," he said. "I think you always have been. Well, you know what they say drugs and alcohol will do to a person."

"I found the barbiturates in your desk."

"So what? The prescription is in your name, prescribed by your physician to relieve anxiety. I was very troubled when I discovered you were mixing them with booze. I even talked to him about it. He was going to hospitalize you for observation, but you disappeared about then. I swear, getting custody of Charlie was a walk in the park."

"If it was such a walk in the park then why did you employ Jodie?"

"I knew nothing about what he did," Jeremy insisted.

"Did you kill him when he failed?"

"I believe he died in a drunk driving accident. Surely you're not blaming me for that, too?"

"You think you've covered all the bases, don't you? Let's try this one. I know about your affair with Valentine Richards."

He leaned back in his chair, a man in his domain, a confident man who could lie without effort. "I suppose you found out about her when you snooped through my files."

"It doesn't matter how I know about her. You were cheating on me. I wonder what your precious community would think of you if they knew that."

"As usual, you have it wrong. Valentine was an intern in my office. Sweet girl. Lost her grandmother while she worked here. I wanted to cheer her up so I sent her flowers."

"You hate flowers."

"But she loved them."

"I love them, too. That never made a difference to you."

"Are you jealous?"

"Oh, please. I just find it interesting that you've finally met someone who makes you think beyond yourself. Maybe you're ready to give me a divorce now."

"No," he said.

"Why?"

He smiled. "Because you want it so badly."

"I don't need your permission," she said.

"If you're hiding from me, it's going to be tricky to show up in court. And oh, then there's that nasty warrant."

Bantering with Jeremy was wasting time. Maybe that was the point. Maybe the police were about to arrive. If that was the case, then she was going to at least see Charlie before it was too late. She walked across the room, grabbed the doorknob and advanced on the staircase.

Jeremy caught her arm and pulled her around. She stumbled on the stair and fell against him. A visceral wave of distaste filled her body as she struggled to stand on her own. He slapped her face so hard her neck snapped to the side. She put a hand up to her stinging cheek and stared into his flat eyes. "Get away from me."

He lowered his head until his mouth was close to her ear. "I could kill you tonight and explain it away however I want. No one on earth would give a damn, not even Charlie, not after a while."

"You never give up, do you, Jeremy. Stop trying to bait me. It doesn't work anymore."

Pounding footsteps from the top of the stairs broke a stalemate. They looked up to see a young woman rushing across the open mezzanine. She stopped short at the head of the stairs and looked down at them.

"What's going on?" Jeremy said.

"It's the boy," the woman responded.

Lily tore herself from Jeremy's gasp and ran up the stairs. Jeremy was right behind her. "What about Charlie?" Lily demanded as she reached the quivering woman who glanced at Jeremy, then back at Lily.

"I've looked everywhere," she said. "He's not in his bed. I don't know… I don't know where he is."

Lily tore down the hall. She entered Charlie's room. It was filled with toys, many of them still in their boxes. The bed was empty. The other two appeared in the doorway as Lily stared at the rumpled sheets. She set her palm against the pillow. It was cool to the touch.

"Is he hiding somewhere? Did he run away?" Jeremy asked.

"I don't know," the woman responded. Lily walked to the window and examined the sill. Then she looked at the wooden window casing. Scratch marks clearly revealed the window had been pried open from the outside. She looked out the open window and saw nothing but the blackness of night. The light that should have illuminated this side of the yard wasn't burning and the moon hadn't yet risen high enough to help.

Her baby had been taken from this room. Had Chance done it? It was possible and if so, at least Charlie was safe. She'd been inside the house for more than thirty minutes, so he could have had time to do this. Her heart slammed against her ribs. Was Chance that rash and impulsive? Yes, at times. But he was smarter than that, she was sure of it. The thought of him trying to help her and actually jeopardizing his freedom—for surely if he had done this and was caught he would wind up in jail—well, it made her sick inside.

"Damn that spoiled brat," Jeremy said under his breath. "If he ran away—"

Lily whirled around, ready to slap him as hard as she could. "How dare you call Charlie—"

"How dare you?" He caught her raised hand and twisted it down to her side but didn't release it. For the first time he seemed to be interested in what she'd been staring at. He pulled her out of his way and turned to examine the window in silence. She knew the gouges on the wood were unmistakable. At last, through clenched teeth, he addressed the other woman. "I employ you to watch my son. You're his damn nanny. Where the hell were you while this was going on?"

"In the other room," she admitted. "I know you said to sit here with him, but my eyes kept drifting closed. I don't know why I'm so blasted sleepy. I knew I had to do something so I went to my room to find a book. I guess I sat down on the bed. The next thing I knew I was yawning myself awake. I wasn't out that long, I swear I wasn't."

"You were gone long enough for this to happen, you nitwit."

"Yes, sir," she said, looking down at the floor. She bent and picked up a piece of paper. "I didn't see this before," she said. "Maybe it fell when I threw back the blankets. Oh, my gosh! It says: *A son for a son. White—*"

Jeremy snatched the paper from the nanny's hand before she read another word. "Give that to me," he said as he released Lily's wrist.

"What does it mean?" Lily demanded. She couldn't believe Chance would leave a message as inflammatory as that. In fact, she knew he wouldn't. That meant someone else had taken Charlie. But who? "Who is White?" she asked.

Jeremy met her gaze but didn't respond, at least not to her. Instead he turned to the nanny. "Get downstairs and tell McCord to search the grounds. I want to know exactly how my son was taken from this room."

She nodded nervously and began to turn. Jeremy cleared his throat. "And Janet? Don't say a word about this to anyone else, do you understand? Not even the police. It's your fault the child is missing. Don't make it worse for yourself by blabbing to anyone but McCord."

"Yes, Mr. Block," she said as she scurried away.

Lily planted her fists on her hips. "What does that note mean, Jeremy? Who is White?"

He looked at the paper again, then folded it in half. "Don't you have enough problems of your own?"

Had he always been this much of a nutcase? Did he really think anything that happened to her mattered in the face of what was happening to their son? "Why aren't you calling the police? And you shouldn't be touching that paper. There may be fingerprints—"

"I will handle this my own way," he interrupted.

"You know something, don't you?" she said in a burst of understanding. "You know who took him and why. Someone named White. Tell me."

The hateful look in his eyes as he raked her over went straight to her gut. He tore the note into pieces and opened his hand to let them flutter to the carpet. She wanted to catch them and paste them back together. She couldn't understand how he could destroy the only link they had to Charlie's abductors.

"It's some enemy of yours, isn't it?" she implored. "Oh, my poor Charlie. How can you stand there and let this happen? Don't you care anything about him? Please—"

He grabbed her shoulders and shook her. "God, you're annoying. I'll get Charlie back safe and sound but I'll do it my own way in my own time. No police. Not unless you want Charlie dead."

Lily swallowed a lump of air. She wasn't sure what to do except get out of that house.

"Now I have to figure out what to do about you," he added.

"No, you don't. I'm leaving."

He stepped in front of her. "I don't trust you. You aren't going anywhere."

"Move out of my way."

"So you can run to the police and in some misdirected gesture of sacrifice, tell them everything you've seen and heard? I'll have to waste time quieting them down and by then it will be too late for Charlie. If you want him to live, you'll stay out of this and you won't involve the police. For now, I have things to do and you're in the way."

His fist connected with her cheekbone and she stumbled backward. Grabbing her arm, he pulled her from the room and all but ran her down the stairs, his fingers digging into her arm. He propelled her into his office, opened the closet, tore her purse from her shoulder and pushed her inside. The door slammed in her face, encasing her in blackness. The click of the lock echoed in her ears.

And then it was silent.

CHANCE WAITED UNTIL he heard the front door close behind Lily and the man she'd called McCord, then jumped over the gate. He dashed to the cover of the trees and hunkered down for a minute as his eyes adjusted to the dark. It seemed odd to him that the outside was so poorly lit but at least he didn't think he had to worry about cameras picking up his every move.

The gun constituted a last-resort measure not to be taken lightly. Bravado aside, he had no intention of shooting anyone if there was any other choice.

Eventually, he knew his sight was as good as it was going to get and he made his way across the manicured lawns to the house where he carefully peered in through a low window. It turned out to be the kitchen—empty. The next window opened onto a dining room that was dominated by a black lacquer table and the most pretentious-looking candelabra he'd ever seen. For a second he stared inside, wondering what bothered him so much, and then he had it. There were two chairs at the table, one at either end, like on a movie set when they wanted you to understand that the people who dined there didn't have much to say to one another.

Had Lily endured dinners in this setting? Chance, who had grown up with four other men and a rotating roster of stepmothers, couldn't imagine the numbing silence and the thought that Charlie might soon eat a peanut-butter-and-jelly sandwich in this mausoleum was just flat-out depressing.

Farther along, he found a living area that looked as though it had never been lived in, and then popped his head up to find himself peering into a smaller room that seemed to be a den or a home office. It, too, appeared empty and he was about to turn away when the chair in the corner suddenly spun around and a man appeared.

Chance immediately ducked out of sight, but the impression of the man stayed vivid behind his eyes: late forties, stern, arrogant. Blue eyes like Charlie's. He held a cell phone in one hand and avidly tapped a pencil against the wooden arm of the chair with another. The window was slightly open, but try as he might, Chance couldn't make out what was being said. He scampered away, careful to keep his head down.

That had to be Lily's husband. But where was Lily? And where was McCord? He decided to skirt the entire perimeter of the house. The harvest moon that had seemed to illuminate the world on his ranch in the middle of the night was subdued here by the massive size of the house and the shadows it cast. Maybe in a couple of hours it would rise high enough to overcome this obstacle, but Chance fervently hoped he and Lily were back in the motel room by then.

And maybe Charlie, too. Maybe Jeremy Block would come to his senses and be reasonable.

Sure. And pigs could fly.

Careful to avoid the patches of light that shone through the windows, he almost tripped when he turned the corner and came across something in the grass. He knelt down to investigate. Someone had left a metal ladder lying on the grass. By the feel and heft of it, a long one.

Why would anyone leave a ladder lying on the grass? He looked up at the bank of windows overhead and saw two lights placed far enough away from each other to suggest two different rooms. Probably upstairs bedrooms; one of those might be Charlie's. He played around with the possibility of raising the ladder and checking it out but decided against it.

Besides, maybe someone had been washing second-story windows today and got lazy or put the ladder down flat so a small boy wouldn't be tempted to climb it and fall. Who knew?

Like a moth drawn to a flame, he retraced his steps to the office window and chanced another peek. This time the door was opening. He shrank back against the rock siding, then slowly inched his face close enough to see inside. Lily stood in front of the desk, her body so taut she almost vibrated. Block stayed seated and managed to look bored as she spoke.

Did he dare nudge the window open farther? No, he decided, too risky. Besides, he could pretty much guess what they were saying. One thing was clear: there was no love lost between them.

After several minutes, Lily turned on her heels and rushed to the door. She ripped it open and slammed it behind her. That was his girl, temper, temper. But Block was out of his chair in a flash, hurrying after her and the look on his face chilled Chance's blood. The door swung closed behind them so whatever happened next occurred without Chance witnessing it. And in his gut he knew nothing good was going on inside that house.

Self-preservation kicked in and he began to wonder where McCord was. If the older man did carry out a cursory patrol of the yard every once in a while, shouldn't he be showing up soon? And exactly how was he going to get out of this yard when the time came to escape? He found the answer to that when he literally ran into a tree growing close to the tall fence. He could shimmy up the trunk and jump down on the other side.

Desperate to know what was going on, Chance crept around to the garage side of the house and smelled smoke. The lights were still off, but he stopped short when he saw the glow of a cigarette as someone sucked on it. Squinting, he could just make out the figure of a man leaning against a white car, an acrid pale cloud hanging in the air around him.

A door opened from the house into a nearby carport. A woman stood framed in the light. "Mr. McCord?" she called with an edge of panic in her voice. She flipped on a weak outside light and McCord pushed himself away from the car and swore.

"Turn the damn light off," he said.

"The little boy is missing! There's a note and everything. Mr. Block said you should find out how the child was taken or if he's still on the grounds. And we're to tell no one about this."

"Have you called the cops?" McCord asked as he emerged into the light. He was a stocky man with an almost bald head.

"Mr. Block insisted no police. He's furious with me."

"What about the kid's mother?"

"Is that who she is? He's furious with her, too. I think he hit her. I better get back inside. Hurry, check the grounds."

She ran back inside the house. Chance expected McCord to turn on the outside floodlights if they had them and sure enough, within seconds the yard jumped from black to living color. He moved at once into one of the few remaining shadows but he had the feeling McCord had witnessed the movement. The older man would come looking and chances were he packed a firearm.

Even more to the point, Lily was apparently trapped inside the house. The maid said Jeremy had hit her. His fists clenched. How badly was she hurt? How could he get her out of there?

Slinking behind a grape arbor still thankfully covered with drooping yellow leaves he could hide behind, he pulled his gun, but paused to try to think.

Who in the world had taken Charlie?

LILY GRASPED OVERHEAD for a light cord to pull. She couldn't find one and there was nothing on the wall. Then she remembered the switch outside the door. The shelves behind her felt like they were covered with office supplies. What could she do when Jeremy returned? Give him a bad paper cut?

She kicked at the door until her foot hurt. She pounded her fists against the heavy wood panel to no avail. She yelled and shouted and had the horrible feeling no one could hear her or that if they did, they would simply ignore her.

Who had taken Charlie and what did they want with him? Her stomach clenched into a knot as she pictured his eyes filled with fear. How could Jeremy be so cavalier about his child's safety? If Jeremy wasn't blowing smoke, then going to the police might prove deadly for Charlie… How did she chance that her lying, cheating husband might actually be telling the truth for once?

She swore under her breath.

A sound on the other side of the door froze her solid for a second and then she frantically started patting the shelves again, feeling for something, anything she could use as a weapon. Her fingers brushed the cool metal of an aerosol can. She grabbed it and another one next to it. She depressed the nozzle sprays and was rewarded with nothing but puffs of air. That's what they were: compressed gas meant to blow the dust from a computer keyboard. Their contents were useless, but they were heavy enough to buy her a moment or two if she used them as projectiles.

The lock clicked and she jumped. This was it. Raising the cans to face height, she squinted against the sudden infusion of light and threw the cans as hard as she could. She opened her eyes in time to see one strike a dark head while a tanned hand caught the other.

"Damn!" Chance said. "Ouch."

"Chance! I'm sorry, I thought you were Jeremy!" She threw herself against him and he caught her, hugging her close for a second, then he raised a hand and gently touched the uninjured part of her cheek. "When I get my hands on that man—"

"Not now," she said. "How did you get in here?"

He gestured at the window. The yard beyond was brilliantly illuminated. "But I don't know how we're going to escape," he said. They heard a yell from outside. "I bet they found the ladder over on the far side of the house. Is that how they took Charlie? Through the window?"

"Yes." She wasn't sure how he knew Charlie was missing but now wasn't the time for conversation.

"We'll have to make a dash for that tree over by the fence. Are you up to it?"

His gaze studied her face and she could imagine what he saw. She knew one eye was swollen because she could feel it with her fingers and she suspected the warm sticky substance on her cheek was blood from Jeremy's last punch. "Don't worry about me," she said. "But Chance, if I'm stopped and you're not, promise me you'll find Charlie."

"Lily…"

"Promise me."

"I promise. Come on."

He stuck his head out the window, then turned to look back at her. "The tree is about twenty feet to your right. Can you climb trees?"

"If I have to."

"Then go. I'll be behind you. I have something to do here."

"What?"

"Lily. Go." He picked her up, and swung her outside.

"See if you can find my purse," she whispered. "It has the car keys."

"Will do." He released her. She dropped to her feet and took off at a dead run. She found the fence and kept going until she got to the tree. Chance showed up earlier than she'd anticipated and hoisted her onto a limb over her head. She scrambled along until she got close to the top of the iron fence and threw herself to the ground on the other side, landing facedown, all but knocking the wind out of her lungs. Chance landed a few seconds after her, but he came down on his feet and absorbed the shock in his legs. He immediately stood and pulled her upright. She saw with relief that he held her purse in one hand.

They ran across the street, thankful to be out of the light.

"I don't know how we avoided being seen," Chance said as Lily led them to the nature trail.

"I don't, either. What did you do in Jeremy's office besides find my purse?"

He pressed her bag into her hands. "Wiped my prints away and kicked in the closet door from the inside. I didn't want your husband knowing you had outside help. You didn't tell him I was with you, did you?"

"No," she said as she extracted the car keys. Would Jeremy believe she was capable of kicking open a door? Maybe, maybe not, but at least he'd wonder.

Lily took the passenger seat. A few seconds later, Chance directed the car onto the quiet road. "Where's the nearest police station?" he asked. The moon illuminated the pavement and they drove without lights for several seconds before they'd turned away from Jeremy's neighborhood and traffic began to appear. The headlights went on and they sped up.

"We're not going to the police," she said.

"But the man hit you, Lily. He locked you in a closet…"

"I'm not important. It's Charlie we have to worry about. Jeremy says if the police get involved, the kidnappers will kill Charlie."

"And you believe him?"

"I don't know what to believe," she said. "But for now, no police. I have to find out who took Charlie. It's someone named White, I think."

"We'll find him," Chance said.

Too caught up in her thoughts, she didn't respond. *A son for a son...* That implied revenge. It had to be tied to Jeremy.

Chapter Four

"Jeremy knows who took Charlie," she said. "And for some reason, he's keeping it to himself, which to me implies he has something to hide." They were digging through the papers Lily had gathered before leaving her husband. The former neat stacks were now in a state of disarray as she grabbed one reprinted article after another. "Look for the death of a man," she coaxed.

Her voice was too highly pitched and the papers seemed to slip through her fingers. Chance wanted to tell her to calm down but he knew better than to even suggest such a thing.

"There was no demand for ransom, right?" Chance asked.

"No."

"Is it possible Jeremy staged the kidnapping to throw you off?"

"Why bother? I'm just a pesky gnat to him."

"Don't underestimate yourself," Chance said. "You can be a hell of a lot more than pesky when you put your mind to it."

"Thanks," she said with a sudden smile.

"What's to keep us from calling the cops?"

"Jeremy said—"

"The man lies as easily as a duck quacks."

"But this time he may be telling the truth. I can't risk it until I know more."

Chance stopped arguing. All it took was one glance at her bruised and bloodied face to make the veins pop in his forehead. No one knew better than he how focused and relentless she could be, but the fact that Jeremy felt he had the right to strike her made his blood boil.

Boiling blood aside, the bigger issue was Charlie. Little Charlie, stolen from his bed, held…well, why? As a hostage? As retribution? What did a five-year-old kid have to make retribution for? Who in the world would take out their hatred for a man on his very young child?

No one sane. Ergo, a lunatic had Charlie. And a lunatic might harm the boy if threatened.

"Here's something," she said, holding up a piece of newspaper. "A man Jeremy prosecuted died of cancer while serving a life sentence. It says, 'Levi Bolt, 68, expired Wednesday—'"

Chance cut her off. "*His* parents would have to be in their eighties. Keep looking."

They fell silent as they searched. "Look at this," she said a few minutes later. He glanced at her face to find that the blood had congealed and her eye had swollen almost closed. He stood up.

"Lily, let me help you clean those wounds."

"Not yet," she said. "Read this to me. It's not long."

He took the paper from her hand and read the article aloud.

"'Police today reported an inmate apparently committed suicide early Saturday morning by hanging himself in his cell. Darke Fallon, estimated age eighteen, was found at 3:25 a.m., January 14. He was being held pending proceedings that were to have started on Monday to determine competency. Prison medical staff attempted life-saving measures before transporting him to Charity Hill Medical Center where he was pronounced dead. Results of toxicology tests were unavailable for review.

"Fallon is accused of the January 10 murder of Mr. Wallace Connor, 21, of Greenville, Idaho, who was found knifed to death in a Boise motel where he had reportedly traveled for a job interview. Twenty-four hours later, police spotted Connor's truck. The driver, Darke Fallon, confessed to the murder but shortly after arrest, ceased cooperating with police. He claimed Connor picked him up while Fallon was hitchhiking from his home in Bend, Oregon, but that could not be confirmed. State appointed attorneys swore to fight demands for hypnosis to establish identity. It is unknown if Mr. Fallon leaves any survivors. The prosecutor's office, headed by Jeremy Block, refused comment.'"

"How could the police not find a trace of him?" Chance mused aloud. "Apparently no fingerprints, no family stepping forward, no Social Security number, no one has ever seen or heard about him before? That seems so unlikely in this day and age."

"I know, I know," Lily said, "But *his* parents would be young enough to steal Charlie."

"If he had any. Did Jeremy talk about this suicide to you?"

"I'm not sure. What's the date again?"

"January 15."

"That's right around the time Jeremy finally knocked me out and I decided to leave. I told you there'd been a suicide at the jail in a cell before he came unglued. This must have been the one."

"Was there a follow-up investigation after his death?"

"Probably."

"There must have been fallout over the suicide," Chance said. "Did you ever hear why the kid killed himself before his trial?"

"No."

Chance skirted through other clippings. "There's nothing else here."

"I'll search the internet," she said, and picking up her phone, went to work. After a half hour they knew a little more but not much.

"Wallace Connor came from Greenville, right? That's pretty close to an area called White Cliff," she finally said. She sat for a moment, then looked up at him. "*White*. Maybe the word *white* in the note wasn't a name of a person but a place." She scanned the screen. "White Cliff appears to be a survivalist community." She groaned and closed her eyes. "Talking kind of hurts," she admitted. "I must have bitten down on the inside of my mouth when Jeremy hit me."

"Wait here," Chance said, and taking the ice bucket, walked to the machine near the outside stairs. Back in the room he gave her a cube to suck on and made a compress by wrapping the rest in a hand towel she held against her face. "I'll take over the search," he added.

"There's a lot in here about that survivalist community you mentioned," he said after he'd continued reading. "One reporter tried to find out if Fallon had ever lived in White Cliff but got nowhere. Apparently the police had the same lack of success."

"How about Wallace Connor?" Lily garbled around the ice cube.

"They say he left behind his parents and a younger

sister. Robbery was the supposed reason for the murder because his wallet was empty and a lapis lazuli ring the desk clerk noticed when he checked in was missing from his hand. The police caught Fallon the next day. He was driving Connor's truck. He told the cops his name, admitted he killed Connor and then shut his mouth and never said another word to anyone about anything. His lawyers were court-appointed. His competency hearing was scheduled for the Monday after he died. His suicide seems to have been the end of it."

"It's a dead end," Lily said bitterly.

He set aside the phone. "No, not a dead end, just a twisty road. We'll figure something out. Come on, let me wash your face and get some antiseptic and a bandage on that open cut. No, don't argue with me." He pulled her up by clasping her arm, grabbed his toiletries kit from his duffel and gently pushed her ahead of him into the bathroom.

She sat on the edge of the tub as he bathed her face in warm water, dabbed on the ointment and covered the open wound with a bandage. The occasional whimpers that escaped her lips made him furious. How dare that jerk touch her.

"Am I pretty again?" she asked as she stood, a little playfulness creeping back into her voice.

He put his hands on her shoulders and studied her face. "Not yet, but you will be."

"Hold me," she said softly.

He drew her closer and put his arms around her. She fit perfectly, as he knew from experience, and though he swore to himself he would not react to her closeness or the way she clung to him, he could feel his body stirring.

"I'm so scared," she whispered against his neck.

He drew back to look at her face, but his gaze landed on her mouth, and mindful of her injuries, he leaned forward and gently touched her lips with his.

They'd kissed a few times several months earlier. To him, her lips had been everything delicious and tasty in the world. Honey and scotch, summer nights, a good dinner. He'd wanted to bed her with a vengeance and had worked on seducing her for weeks, but one torrid fifteen minutes had led to her bolting away from him for good.

So what? There were more women in the world than men and he'd known his share. Frankly, he seemed to have a knack for finding women who wanted what he wanted—a satisfying romp in the hay, no heartstrings engaged. His father had been married seven times. Seven times! Women came and went, the trick was not to block the door.

And then came Lily.

Tricky, complicated, troubled, on the run, dangerous.

She pulled away from him and studied his face. "Thank you for rescuing me from the closet."

"You're welcome." He touched her good cheek. Her skin was so soft.

She nodded briskly and disengaged herself from his embrace. He longed to keep his fingers linked behind her back, longed to hold her in his arms all night. He knew she was distracted and sick with worry and so was he... *Oh, give it up*, his brain scolded, and he withdrew his hands.

"We need to talk to those survivalists ourselves," he said as they returned to the room. He looked away from the bed, which suddenly seemed to take up almost all the floor space. She sat down in the chair in front of the table and shook her head. "I know. It's wild land up there, people are scattered and many are suspicious of outsiders. I guess we start by finding White Cliff."

"Yeah," he said. His voice sounded too loud.

"I'm going to go back over everything in the files. We must have missed something," she said.

"Now?"

"Right now."

He shook his head. "It's late, Lily. You need sleep. There's always tomorrow…"

"You go ahead," she said, her attention on the papers she held in her hands. "I'm not sleepy yet."

Maybe she didn't want to crawl into bed with him. Maybe that was too risky for her. He stripped off his clothes and got under the covers, noting as he did all this that she didn't look at him once. Man, as soon as Charlie was safe, he had to somehow get to her.

He knew he couldn't sleep even though she'd switched off most of the lamps. A few minutes later when he glanced at her, he found her sitting in the sole pool of light, head bent over the table, a solitary figure obsessed and afraid. He sat up and reached out to touch her shoulder and she pulled away. He laid his head back on the pillow to consider what his next move should be. Against all odds, he fell asleep instead.

THE WORDS BEGAN to blur in Lily's eyes. There was just so much unrelated stuff. Copies of papers detailing Jeremy's courtroom victories, memos to office staff including several to Valentine Richards, who apparently worked for Jeremy just as he claimed, which didn't preclude a personal relationship. Still, maybe lightning struck twice tonight. Maybe he'd told the truth about Valentine and the danger of police involvement, too.

And so what if they'd had an affair? She should have known it wouldn't matter. Going to his house thinking the knowledge of his infidelity would give her leverage seemed terribly naive in retrospect. And Chance had warned her but she hadn't had any other options so she'd refused to listen.

Where was her boy? How did she keep breathing not knowing if he was in danger? *Keep focused…* She found receipts from the dry cleaner's and the bakery and the shoe store. There were photographs as well: a large boat, the day's catch from some fishing trip, buildings she didn't recognize, women wearing suggestive clothing…

Oh, what was the point of all of this?

She got up and paced. Chance's breathing was steady and deep—he was down for the count. The thought of sitting here for seven more hours while Charlie was in trouble made her shiver inside.

And then she knew that she couldn't wait, not another minute. Working quickly but quietly, she gathered all of the papers and stuffed them back in their envelope. She sat down to write Chance a note explaining why she had to leave and why it was better if she went alone.

It wasn't fair to keep dragging him into the minefield her life had become. She knew what he wanted from her—a quick, easy fling that would be over for him the moment it became real for her.

But it was more than that. She was asking him to climb out on a limb with her because she had no intention of returning Charlie to Jeremy. She would be on the run forever and Chance was a guy with roots so deep they touched the center of the earth which was, for him, his three brothers, his father and a ranch that had been in the family's hands for over a hundred years.

Now that she'd made up her mind to go off on her own, it was clear she should never have allowed him to accompany her even this far. She reread her note. It all sounded like a lot of half-baked excuses.

She looked back into the room before closing the door, half hoping Chance would stir, that he'd sit up, that he'd see her, but his breathing remained steady, his body still. She whispered goodbye under her breath and closed the door behind her. She drove away without looking back, certain she was doing the logical, reasonable, all-around best thing for everyone. It had to be right because it felt so terrible...

CHANCE WOKE UP, yawned, then sat up abruptly.

There was no sign of Lily.

"Damn," he swore under his breath. Why in the world had he chosen now to turn into Rip Van Winkle?

He got out of bed and dressed in a hurry, looking around as he pulled on his boots. Not only was Lily not in the room, there was no sign she ever had been. She'd taken everything with her.

"Damn," he said again. He tucked his gun out of sight under his shirt and opened the outside door. Morning light seemed to shine straight down on the empty spot where he'd parked her car the night before.

For a second he tried to tell himself she'd gone out to bring back breakfast, but he knew it wasn't true. There was a total feeling of abandonment. She was gone.

Back inside, he searched every horizontal surface for a note that might explain why she'd run out on him...again. He finally spied a wadded-up piece of paper in the garbage can and sat down as he smoothed open the paper.

After reading the first sentence, he swore under his

breath and stood. A minute after that, he picked up his duffel bag and locked the room behind him.

IT TOOK HIM six hours to hitchhike the two hundred miles home and that was because he was eventually lucky enough to catch a ride with a guy who lived in Falls Bluff. Once in town, he walked to the feed store where he knew Patty Reed, the pigtailed girl who worked behind the counter, would lend him her truck so he could drive himself home.

However, she did more than that. She actually insisted on getting someone to cover for her and driving him herself. Chance knew this had little to do with his own charisma; Patty was hot for Chance's younger brother, Pike. However, a ride was a ride.

They arrived at the ranch house to find his father and his new stepmother, Grace, still off in Oregon. Gerard and Pike were unloading bales of hay into the feed barn using a combination of brute strength and a forklift to get the job done. Kinsey had not yet returned from New Orleans, though Gerard had pinned many of her rough sketches to the walls in the barn because he liked looking at them. Horses peered over a fence; a looming tree sat alone on a hilltop. A herd of deer grazed in a field at twilight. There was even one of the ghost town that existed on ranch property, and though it had been the site of tragedy for Gerard, it was situated front and center. Maybe it was his way of domesticating the pain, of reclaiming good memories as well as bad.

Gerard told Chance that Kinsey had made this switch from portraiture to scenery and still life because she'd finally found a real family to belong to: theirs, and a real home in which to plant roots. Seeing as she and

Gerard were going to be married next summer, it made perfect sense.

Gerard, busy driving the forklift, looked up as Chance walked into the barn followed by Patty who immediately veered over toward Pike and leaned fetchingly nearby. Chance supposed his scholarly-looking brother made an attractive picture to a kid barely out of high school. Lots of girls thought glasses made a guy look smart. It didn't hurt that in Pike's case, he could back up the advertising with an agile brain.

"You leave with one girl and come back with another," Gerard said as he turned off the noisy machine.

"I just caught a ride with Patty. She's here to ogle Pike."

They both looked over at the truck. Pike seemed to be ignoring the girl.

"He's preoccupied right now," Gerard said. "His mom in LA called this morning. There's some issue with his stepsister."

"You know," Chance said, "every once in a while, I kind of wish we all had the same mother instead of different ones, but then I think she might have been like Pike's and I'm okay with things the way they are."

"No kidding," Gerard said. "Where's Lily? What happened? She's not really in jail, is she?"

"Not yet," Chance said and gave Gerard an abbreviated explanation of the past twenty-four hours.

"Charlie is missing? Again? Lily must be worried sick. Even that louse of a husband has to be concerned."

"I don't know. He seems to know more than he's telling. Lily said he acted as though he knew exactly who had the boy. The word *white* was mentioned in the note. We thought it was a name at first but it's also a survivalist camp or something up in the panhandle. It might be that someone from there took Charlie or it could be a complete red herring."

"You let her go off alone to a survivalist's enclave?"

"Enclave?"

"Yeah. White Cliff isn't just a camp, it's an unincorporated community. There are lots of places like it across the country. This one is dominated by a guy named Robert Brighton. He and the others call themselves true patriots, devoted to knowing how to defend and take care of themselves in the event of a military or natural catastrophe."

"I'd never heard of it before yesterday. How do you know so much?"

Gerard shrugged. "Remember Gary Stills from high school?"

"Sure."

"He got disgusted with rising taxes and government involvement in their ranch a few years back and took his wife and kid and moved up that way. I heard from him a year or so ago. He ranted on about getting ready for Armageddon so I read up on it."

"Hell, it's hard to imagine Lily in that kind of situation," Chance said, wondering how in the world she expected to uncover anything on her own. "And it's hard to believe those people would kidnap a little boy and subject themselves to police involvement. They don't sound like the type."

"As long as you don't cross them. Anyway, you said Lily's husband refuses to involve the police so they have little to worry about."

"Yeah, and how exactly did they know he'd react that way? It seems totally out of character for him. If all he's interested in is free press and sympathetic votes, why doesn't he jump on this chance to get his son's plight on every news channel in the country?"

"All good questions," Gerard said. "When are you joining Lily?"

Chance took off his hat and pulled it on again. "I'm not."

Gerard stared at him, his brilliant blue eyes thoughtful.

"Don't look at me like that," Chance protested. "She left me high and dry. I don't even know for sure she went to White Cliff. She might have found another lead after I went to bed."

"Why did she go alone?"

"She said something about not wanting to involve me. If that's the way she wants it, then fine."

"I guess it's out of your hands," Gerard said. "It's her son, right? Well," he added as he turned the forklift back on, "I'd better get back to work. Pike is waiting on me."

Chance took a deep breath. "I'll go help him. After a day with Lily, picking up bales of hay will be child's play."

By nightfall, he'd worked until his muscles ached. Unfortunately, they weren't the only parts of him that hurt. He went outside the main ranch house where he'd decided to spend the night. If that was the phone number Charlie knew, then it was best there be somebody here to answer it. He sat on the bench, breathing in the cold autumn air. Forty-eight hours before, Lily had driven back into his life.

A vehicle pulled into the parking area and he stood abruptly. Had she had second thoughts? Seconds later, the headlights dimmed, the door opened. And then he recognized Pike's lean frame walk toward him as the interior light peeking through the open door sparkled against his glasses. As usual, the dogs provided an escort.

Swallowing disappointment, he sat back down on the bench. "How's it going?" Pike asked as he leaned against the railing.

"Okay. Gerard said you heard from Mona. She all right?"

"My mother is never all right, you know that," Pike said. "The woman isn't alive unless she's neck deep in drama. Her boyfriend seems to have cheated on her."

"Gerard also mentioned Tess."

"Yeah. Apparently when she heard about what her father had done, she stormed off. She's only eighteen, you know, and LA can be a rough place when you're alone."

"I met her the summer before last when you flew her here for a visit. She's a smart kid."

"I guess," Pike said.

"Yeah. Well, I know you're worried about her,". Even in the half-light, he could see the strain on Pike's face.

"Yeah." He took off his glasses and pinched the bridge of his nose. "But you know how I feel. Maybe you're inexperienced when it comes to worrying about a little sister, but you're positively preoccupied with Lily."

"No, I'm not," Chance said.

Pike's eyebrows inched up his forehead.

"No, really," Chance insisted. "She's made it clear she thinks I'm a bumbling oaf. I could save that woman's life once a day from now until hell froze over, and she'd still second-guess everything I did or said."

"That doesn't sound like you," Pike said.

"What do you mean?"

"Since when do you let anyone scare you away?"

"You know Lily. She's a lot easier to look at than to deal with."

"Maybe. I just keep thinking about Charlie."

As if on cue, the phone rang. Chance hurried inside and picked up on the second ring. "Yes," he said, tense with anticipation.

But the call was from one of his father's friends. Chance disconnected and went back outside where the sound of the nearby river rushing over rocks mimicked his hammering heart. Why was he so disappointed that the call hadn't been from someone in trouble? Was he a ghoul?

No, he decided. But sitting here on the ranch waiting to hear if Charlie was okay, not knowing what was going on…it was eating him up inside.

"I'm going to bed," he announced.

"Sounds like a good idea," Pike said, and getting to his feet, ambled back to the truck. Chance locked the door and climbed the stairs.

After four hours of lying on his back and staring at the moonlit ceiling, he swore under his breath. He sat up and walked downstairs, stared at the silent phone, then grabbed his tablet computer and went back on the internet where he eventually found a reference to White Cliff that called the proposed community a fortress. Sounded formidable. It couldn't be that hard to find, could it?

Well, it was wild country and a lot bigger than it appeared on a map. You could drive down endless unpaved forest roads if you didn't know which to take…

There was only one person Chance could think of who might be able to help. But why would Jeremy Block offer any information? He wouldn't. Chance needed a bargaining tool. Did they have anything in common? No, nothing, except maybe Lily.

Lily. It always came back to her.

He put down the tablet and walked outside. For a minute, he let his mind wander the ranch. The fields, the big old hanging tree, the ghost town, the generations of people who had lived and worked, ranched and mined, fished the rivers and hunted for food, built homes, given birth and gasped their last breath right on this land. Sounds of the river filled the night. A horse whinnied nearby. The ponderous full moon stared down at him. Wind rustled the boughs overhead. The ranch was peaceful on this autumn night, demanding nothing. Come first light, another busy day of ranching would commence. The list of things to do stretched on for eternity. This was his life, his home.

"Damn her," he muttered yet again.

It was too early to make any phone calls, but it wasn't too early to go home and pack a bag. He left a note on the board for his brothers and took off for his own cabin. A half hour after that, dressed in the clothes he'd worked in all day, he tucked the handgun and a rifle into a locked case behind the seat of the oldest vehicle on the ranch, a thirty-year-old Ford pickup. He wanted to look inconspicuous. He wanted to be able to change his story whenever he needed to, be invisible or all over the map.

The cattle guard rumbled a goodbye as he drove off Hastings land and headed south. It was time to be someone else for a while, time to go undercover.

Chapter Five

Chance had debated how to present himself. Unkempt, drunk, angry? Somehow he doubted any one of those alone would work on Block. But crafty and sneaky wouldn't work, either. He decided on a mix of characteristics and knew he would depend mostly on luck.

He parked the truck on the other end of the path he and Lily had used to escape and locked his wallet in the box with the guns. He wasn't sure what he would find at the Block house and he didn't want any ties to the Hastings name. What he knew was that going off to northern Idaho without knowing what Jeremy Block had already set in motion was too dangerous. Chance didn't want to get blindsided but even more than that, he didn't want Charlie caught in the middle of a situation where everyone around was armed to the teeth.

Maybe Block wouldn't be home. Maybe he'd gone after his kid. That would be good to know, as well, because if Lily got in Block's way, she was toast.

McCord didn't show up at the gate so Chance marched up to the front door, punched the doorbell three times fast in a row with his knuckle and banged his fist against the dark wood. No prints in knuckles and fists. This guy was a DA with law enforcement ties and Chance did not want to leave any tangible proof of his identity behind.

The door was opened by the woman Chance had seen come to the kitchen door to tell McCord that Charlie had disappeared.

He took a deep breath. Showtime.

Before she could utter a word, he pushed the door open with his shoulder and barged past her. "Where is she?" he demanded. He strode to the stairs and started to climb them, hollering, "Lily?" at the top of his lungs. Hopefully Jeremy Block was somewhere in the house and would hear him.

A door behind him opened and Chance turned to see the man he'd glimpsed through the window "What in the hell is going on?" he demanded.

"Where is she?" Chance said, coming back down the stairs. "I know she's here."

"Where is who?"

"Lily Kirk. She talked about you sometimes. Is she here?"

Block cut him off with a barking laugh. "That woman is poison."

"Amen."

"And I should know, I'm married to her."

Chance allowed his expression to register surprise. He made a big deal of looking around the opulent surroundings and whistling low in his throat. "I knew she'd lived with you and all but she never said a word about being married. Brother, I can't believe she ran out on all this. I didn't know she was that stupid."

Block seemed to suddenly notice that the woman who had opened the door was still standing nearby. "For heaven's sake, Janet, close the door and get lost," he commanded. She did as he asked and hurried up the stairs, giving Chance a wide berth,

"Just tell me. Is the bitch here or not?" Chance demanded.

"Come into my office," Block said. "Let's have a civilized drink and discuss this." Chance preceded him into the den. He paused to stare at the closet door he'd splintered two nights before. "What happened?"

"Nothing important," Block said but his teeth stretched tight over his teeth as though tasting something bitter. "What's your name?"

"Pete Reed," Chance said, digging up the moniker of an old school pal. "At least that's the name I'm using right now. My real name is none of your business."

"Why are you so angry with Lily?"

"She stole two thousand three hundred bucks from me, money I had to get from a guy who is twice as mean as anybody I ever served with in the army. The dude almost killed me but I got what he owed me, I always do. And then that bitch stole it."

"You're really mad," Block said.

"Hell, yes, I'm mad."

Block narrowed his eyes as though assessing what he was seeing. "How mad?"

"Mad enough to make her wish she'd never met me."

"She has that effect on men," Block said. "Have you ever done any time?"

"Twice. Trumped-up assault charges. I was a little out of sorts after my discharge from the army. I've got a temper, I admit it."

"Where do you work now?"

Chance emphasized an impatient sigh. "I was a bouncer at a strip club until I blew town to find Lily.

How is this getting me any closer to that goal and why the third degree?"

"You a good shot?"

"Give me a gun and a knothole a hundred yards away and I'll show you."

Block poured two small glasses of amber liquor out of a crystal decanter he kept on the desk and handed one to Chance. "Cheers," he said, hoisting his glass to his lips. Chance did the same and downed it in one gulp, trying to get a handle on where Block was coming from. He sure didn't act like a guy whose kid had been taken.

Block sat behind his desk and motioned for Chance to take a seat opposite him. "If I know Lily, and I do, she's trying to get our son back."

"Charlie?"

"You know the boy?"

"Sure, I saw him around now and again. Lily didn't encourage us to be friendly if you know what I mean." He grinned and added, "Maybe she thought I'd be a bad influence. Who is she trying to get him back from? You?"

"No. I had him for a day or two but then someone stole him away in the night."

"So that's why she left Reno? Because someone took Charlie from her?"

"Yes. Me."

Chance looked around again. "The kid will be better off here than in that dump in Reno."

"Of course he will. But a third party decided they wanted to hurt me so they took Charlie."

Chance shook his head. "I don't get it. Why isn't this place swarming with cops? What kind of ransom do they want?"

"No ransom demand has been made and I didn't call

the police. I don't want them involved. Too dangerous. What I want to do is steal him back."

"Then go do it. If he were my kid I wouldn't be sitting here yapping about it."

Block's lip curled in anger but he quickly covered it with a self-deprecating smile. "I can't. If I show up, who knows what they'll do to the boy. I need someone else to take care of it. Maybe someone like you."

"Me?" Chance scoffed. "Ha." He paused as though thinking and added. "If they don't want money for the kid, then why did they take him?"

"I have no idea," Block said. *Like hell you don't,* Chance thought. "The only thing I have to go on is a note they left. That's why I'm pretty sure where he is."

"And where's the note?"

"Lily took it with her when she left," he said. No trace of the lie he'd just told surfaced in his eyes. "But like I said, she'll charge in and mess up everything."

"A specialty of hers," Chance said. "But I still don't see how any of this gets me closer to my money."

"I'm going to be honest with you," Block said. "I need help. I need someone I can trust—"

Chance shot to his feet and laughed. "Trust? Hell, you don't even know me."

"Sit down, Pete, please. I'm an excellent judge of character."

Chance grabbed his glass and gestured at the decanter. The glass he could break before he left, but he didn't want his prints on the liquor bottle. Block took the hint and poured him a shot that Chance knocked back as he reclaimed the chair. "You want me to go get him, is that it?"

"Yes."

Chance stared at Block, who didn't flinch. After a long

pause, he shook his head again. "Excuse me, but looking around it's hard not to notice you must be loaded. Hell, hire yourself a private detective."

"Listen to me, Pete, it isn't that simple. These aren't ordinary people. It's going to take someone with finesse and cunning and you strike me as a man with both those qualities."

"Flattery won't get you anywhere," Chance said. "Use one of your own people."

"I had to fire the only man I would trust with a job like this."

"Why'd you fire him?"

"He failed to protect my son and I do not tolerate failure. Listen, just come up with a convincing story, fit in for a few days and then when the time is right, do what needs to be done and extract my kid without getting him hurt."

"Lily will know I'm ready to do whatever I have to in order to get my money back. If she's there, she'll turn me in as a liar the moment she sets eyes on me."

"Not if you take care of her first thing," Block said softly.

Chance had come here hoping to get a lead on finding Charlie and by default, Lily. But he wasn't prepared for what he thought he'd just heard. "Are you talking about killing her?" he said.

Block shrugged. "I have a bottle of her barbiturates. Assuming she's there, all you have to do is get the pills down her throat. It will appear she committed suicide. But if something goes wrong and she does finger you, off you go, no harm, no foul." He cleared his throat. "I don't expect you to risk yourself for nothing. I'll give you what she stole from you and a bonus, too. If she still has your cash on her it might be best to leave it with her so no one gets suspicious. When you bring Charlie back to me, I'll add another twenty grand."

Chance whistled. "Murder, though. I haven't killed anyone since the army."

"And you did it then because you were fighting a war. This is war, too. The victory is freeing a child. Do you have a gun?"

"Not on me, but I can get one. Where do I find Lily and all the rest of these people?"

"An area called White Cliff."

Bingo, Chance thought. Confirmation. Lily was right. Hell, she often was which was just another irritating thing about her. "Where's that?"

"Up in Idaho's panhandle, almost to the border. It's one of those commune things. The leader is a guy named Roberts. He's a fast talker and a hard hitter but I heard he's not around the place as much as he used to be. There's a woman up there who runs a small store located outside the walls of the community. She calls herself Maria Eastern. If Charlie is living there, she'll know about it. You can't ask her straight out, though, and you can't mention my name or she'll put a bullet through your brain."

"The price just went up ten thousand," Chance said. Block opened his mouth to speak but closed it without saying anything. "And I'm going to need more cash up front," Chance added. "I have to buy the gun I told you about and my truck needs a tire. I don't plan on spending my own money."

"I'll add another thousand," Block said.

"Two thousand," Chance countered.

Block gritted his teeth. "Be warned that these people are heavily armed and know how to handle themselves."

"Sure."

"Wait for me in the entry."

Chance had already folded the tiny shot glass in his fist and took it with him when he left the office. Block soon appeared and handed over an open envelope stuffed with cash Chance assumed he'd retrieved from a hidden safe inside the office. There was also a slip of paper with a crude map naming roads and estimated distances. In the end he was supposed to look for a red no-trespassing sign.

"There are going to be a million of those," Chance said without touching the note.

"Look at the spelling."

Trespassing had been spelled *tresspassing*. "That's intentional," Block added. "That's the sign that points out the right road or so I'm told."

"Is this place some kind of secret?"

"Not at all. It's located close to a town called Greenville but the less you show your face or ask directions, the better for you if things go wrong."

Chance stuffed the envelope of money in his pocket. "You must really love that kid," he said.

"He is my son. Once I have him back, I won't lose him again even if I have to send him out of the country to school."

"Then nobody better get caught," Chance said, implying, he hoped, that this meant him, too.

"You'd be smart to keep something in mind," Block said. "I'm an important man in this state. If it comes to whose word will be believed, it will be mine, not yours. If you double-cross me, I'll find you."

So much for all that baloney about trust. On the other hand, Chance didn't have to pretend to feel the chill in Block's icy gaze. His fear did not originate from concerns for himself. It was Lily and Charlie he worried about. The fact the tough older guy wasn't at the house was troublesome, too, as was the quick way Block had bought and enhanced Chance's original scheme, almost as though he'd read the script beforehand.

Was it possible he knew who Chance really was? Could this be a trap? Was he being played by the guy he was playing?

And where was McCord?

Block opened the front door. At the last second, he caught Chance's arm and Chance turned. "Don't forget this," he said, pressing a prescription bottle into Chance's hand. "And be sure to give Lily my best."

Chance took the crystal shot glass out of his pocket where he'd wiped it clean on a bandana. "Thanks for the drinks," he said and walked away.

THE DRIVE WAS long and lonely and it was dark by the time Chance finally found the misspelled sign along with an arrow pointing down a dark tunnel of unpaved road and huge trees. After a mile or two, he came across a small community of very old houses where only a few looked inhabited. The rest were falling apart with sunken porch roofs and moss-covered fences. There was a small store on the other side of the road that looked downright festive in comparison, seeing as it had a neon soda sign in the window and a big old ice machine out front. It appeared to still be open.

Chance itched to stop there, for perhaps that was Maria Eastern's store. But first he wanted a glimpse of White Cliff. All the internet had had to offer were artists' drawings of walls and buildings. He had no idea how much if anything actually existed. If it was in the same state of disrepair as this little settlement, then everyone was barking up the wrong tree.

A half mile farther along the road, he came upon a wide spot backed by a nine-foot-high rock wall. He got out of the truck but left the headlights burning. That old moon he was so fond of shone enough that he could tell a huge area of land had been cleared beyond the wall. Other than that, all he could see was fence. There was no sign announcing that this was White Cliff but what else could it be? Well, the gate in the wall was firmly closed so there was no use standing there staring at it. Tomorrow he'd have to find a way inside.

Back in the truck, he retraced his route to the store, this time noticing another sign pointing out a place called Freedom Lake. The road was an offshoot of the one he was on, consisting of heavily rutted dirt and ghostly looking trees.

The parking lot at the store was empty but an open sign hung in the door so he went inside. A gangly young man with dark hair cut very short stood behind the counter, flipping through the pages of a catalog. He wore a camouflage long-sleeved shirt.

"Howdy," Chance said.

The kid nodded once and went back to his catalog. Chance grabbed a can of juice from the refrigerator section and a package of chips off a rack. When he got to the counter, the kid registered his purchases with a disinterested flicker of his eyes, punched in some numbers and gave Chance a total.

"It's pretty country up here," Chance said as he counted out the money. "Real peaceful." He glanced at the catalog, which was open to a page dedicated to shotguns. "I bet you do a lot of hunting up this way."

"Yeah," the kid said. He didn't look much over seventeen, maybe not even that old.

Chance gestured at the catalog. "When I was about your age, my dad got me a BB gun."

"That's for little kids," the boy scoffed.

"I guess. I had fun with it though. Until I killed my first songbird. Didn't feel too macho over that."

"Killing animals for sport is wrong," the boy said. He picked up the catalog and turned to an earmarked page. "This is my next gun. I've almost saved enough to buy it." The item he pointed to was an assault rifle.

"That's not really a hunting gun," Chance murmured.

"No siree, but if you have trouble with people, this is the weapon you want."

"And your parents will let you buy it?"

"It's just Mom, my brother and me. And sure, she doesn't care. I've been proficient with automatic rifles since I was twelve. In fact, I can shoot a human-size target nine out of ten shots."

"I'm impressed," Chance said.

The kid smiled. "It's no big deal. Everyone in White Cliff over the age of thirteen has to be able to do that. And you have to qualify with a handgun, too. You know, in case."

Chance opened the bag of chips and offered them to the boy who took a couple with a shy grin and a hasty thanks. "Mom won't let me eat the junk food we sell in here. If we can't kill it ourselves or grow it, we barter for it."

"Sometimes there's nothing like a bag of salty goodness," Chance said.

"Yeah. My favorite are pretzels. My aunt bakes them herself, but they're not the same. My cousin used to have a thing for sunflower seeds. His mom planted whole rows of plants in the garden, but sometimes, I'd smuggle him a bag or two from the store."

Chance laughed and offered more chips. "Do you have a large family?"

"Not that big. Now it's just my mom and brother and a bunch of step-cousins and an aunt and a uncle, you know."

"Sure. You said you needed to be proficient with a weapon just in case. In case of what?"

The boy swallowed his chips and took a few more. "Well, let's say terrorists knock out our country's power grid," he said. "Everything crashes. Everything. Your money in the bank is gone in the blink of an eye. Pretty soon you run out of food and gasoline and everything else. You got no electricity to keep your freezer running. You can't trust your city's water. But us here at White Cliff won't be affected because we're preppers."

"Preppers?" Chance said.

"Yeah. That's just a name for people who prepare for the inevitable trouble ahead. You know, we stockpile food and ammo. We take care of ourselves. Anyway, so all those panicked people start trying to take what we have and they're so scared, they're dangerous. We need to be able to protect ourselves."

"That sounds reasonable," Chance said but he had to suppress a shiver. The thought of children shooting other children to protect their food was nauseating.

"Or say the government decides to impose undemocratic laws and come after us for no reason? I mean, it could happen. Heck, we just got a new teacher at the school whose uncle was gunned down in Texas a few years back by a government agency."

"How many people live up there?

"A couple hundred. Maybe more like three now but someday it will have thousands. We have our own stores and schools and just about everything a person needs."

"Do you know a family by the name of Fallon?"

The boy ate the last chip and brushed the salt off his hands. Chance offered him the unopened juice and he took it with a nod of appreciation. "You're talking about that guy who murdered a Greenville man down in Boise."

"You know about that?"

"Sure. Police came and asked questions. Everyone knows about him up here but nobody had ever seen him and there's no trace of him having a family here or in Greenville, either." He opened the juice and took a long swallow.

A noise at the door made the kid look up and Chance turn round. A woman wearing a long black coat entered. The boy slammed the can down on the counter and whipped the empty bag off to the side. The woman watched him do both, a suspicious frown twisting her lips for a second. "Dennis? What are you doing?"

"Nothing, Mom," he said.

The woman was tall and stern-looking with very straight graying black hair that fell almost to her waist, dark eyes and an old scar on her forehead.

"Best you go on home now, I'll close up the store," she said, sparing Chance a lingering perusal as she strode around the counter. The kid grabbed his jacket from the back of a chair, stuffed the rolled-up catalog into a pocket and hurried out of the store without looking at Chance again.

Chance offered the woman his hand. "Pete Reed," he said. "You have a nice boy."

"Maria Eastern," she replied. "I know he's nice. Too nice, sometimes. He needs to know when to keep his mouth closed. People take advantage of innocence." She took off her coat and hung it on a hook. She was almost as tall as his six feet one inch. "What are you, one of those reporters come sniffing around for a story?"

"No," Chance said. "Do you get a lot of reporters up here?"

"Some. Mostly they treat White Cliff as a novelty."

"I did drive up to the end of the road when I first got here," he said. "I wanted to look around but the gate appeared to be locked."

"It's late," she said. "We tend to rise and set with the sun in these parts and we don't like strangers driving by our homes after dark."

Or any other time, he bargained. "I used to know some people who moved up this way. Their last name is Fallon. Do you know them?"

"Are you sure you're not a reporter?" she asked, her hooded eyes veiled.

"I'm sure."

"There is no one named Fallon here and never has been."

He needed to up the ante and give himself a reason to hang around. "It was just a thought. Listen, ma'am, I'm sure you don't want to hear my story, but I was living on land my grandfather homesteaded and when my daddy died the government took so many taxes we had to sell off half the land just to stay out of the slammer. I told them those were the last taxes they were taking from me and now they've taken everything except the cash in the ground. My woman used to talk about relocating to

White Cliff, but I always had my family's land to consider. Now that's gone and so is she. I've got nothing."

"And what do you want from us?"

"A fresh start. I just want to look around. I dug up the last of the money Grandpa buried under a rock and it's just enough to buy a place up here. Maybe if Dorrie hears I've turned myself around she'll come back to me."

Maria stared hard at him with those dark, dark eyes. Her vision seemed to snake through his skin, along his arteries, straight to his lying heart. "I'll think about what you've said," she finally muttered. "We take turns at White Cliff dealing with interested parties who show up on our doorstep. This week it's my turn. Come back here about one o'clock tomorrow. But I should tell you that I can often see through lies and self-delusion. I've had a lot of practice. So, I suggest you spend your night being honest with yourself and tomorrow being honest with me."

Her comment surprised him. "I'll do that," he said. What would happen if he was honest with her right now? If he asked if Lily had shown up, if he asked about Charlie being here, if he admitted he was scamming Jeremy Block?

And risk a bullet to the brain?

He needed to think about this. He left the store without saying another word and drove slowly back to the last town he'd driven through to find a motel.

Something told him he was in for another sleepless night.

Chapter Six

Okay, she'd done it. She'd found White Cliff, she'd come up with a convincing story to elicit enough sympathy to buy her a few days' hospitality and even managed to ingratiate herself into the community by volunteering to take over a fifth-grade class for an ailing teacher. All this in a little over thirty hours. Not bad.

She looked around the small room of ten-year-olds. One student stood in front of her desk reading aloud from a history book. This particular volume had been published sixty years earlier and there was the taint of revisionist history in the curriculum, but the kids sat calmly at their desks and appeared to listen.

A beautiful new school was under construction next door and the sound of hammers and saws made their way through the windows. Most importantly, Lily had learned that a kindergarten class was held in the adjacent building. Her plan was to dash down there and check it out as soon as her class went to what the school called recess but which she'd learned consisted of laps around the track.

She had one goal: find Charlie. If he was here, it figured he'd be in that kindergarten class, sitting right out in the wide-open. She was hoping the fortress nature of this place might breed complacency. When you are surrounded by like-minded people who all know and support you, to say nothing of two walls between you and the rest of the world, it might be easy to assume you were safe.

She could see why someone would exact revenge against Jeremy—boy, could she. She could even see why they might go so far as to kidnap his son if they felt he'd "kidnapped" theirs by facilitating his death. What fueled the anxiety eating at her gut was that revenge would go too far and Charlie would become part of some insane sacrifice.

Her subtle attempt to find out if someone had recently "acquired" a five-year-old boy had been thoroughly ignored. She was afraid to mention Darke Fallon or Wallace Connor, afraid to push too hard. It was all so frustrating. She had to struggle every minute not to begin pounding on doors or give in to the longing to call the FBI and beg them to find her son.

What would Chance do? For a second she remembered him as she'd last seen him, asleep and peaceful. In another life, if they'd met first, maybe they could have found a way to build a future. Even if she'd managed to leave Jeremy in such a way that he hadn't decided killing her was preferable to divorcing her, she might still have found Chance and then she and Charlie could live with him and play with him and work with him…and love him.

She finally realized the whole classroom had fallen silent, including the child who had apparently finished reading. With horror, she felt a tear sting the gash on her cheek as it rolled down her face.

"Sorry about that, kids," she said. "I was thinking about our country's…great history. I guess I got emotional. Emma, you read the chapter very well. It's almost time to go run around the field a couple of times. Be back in twenty minutes."

The kids got up eagerly and filed out of the classroom. Lily made herself sit there for a moment in case one of them came back for something, and then she got to her feet and walked briskly down the hall toward the door. She crossed a small courtyard and opened another door directly into the kindergarten room. Her hope she could spy on the class without being seen evaporated as more than a dozen kids and two adults turned to face her.

Her gaze swept the children as her heart almost beat out of her chest. Several were blond—none were Charlie.

"May we help you?" one of the women asked. Lily had been told all the teachers were parents who took turns teaching the kids who attended this organized school but many parents chose to homeschool their kids themselves in their own homes. She told herself that Charlie might be with such a family; his not being here didn't absolutely mean he wasn't at White Cliff.

"Sorry to barge in," she said. "I'm new and I was just looking around. I thought this doorway led to the restrooms."

The other woman spoke up. "They're in the main building."

"Thanks," Lily called and left the classroom. She returned to her own class to finish the teaching day but she did so with a heavy heart. Where was Charlie and what did she do now?

MARIA TOLD CHANCE she'd decided to give him a personal tour and he could leave his truck parked outside the wall. He wasn't flattered by her attention—he figured it had more to do with keeping an eye on him than because she liked his company. She drove him around the perimeter first and he was duly impressed by the organization set out in front of him.

As she drove, she delivered a well-rehearsed spiel about the community being the vision of a solitary man. Since his death, his son, Robert Brighton, had assumed leadership. Chance saw signs of building going on everywhere.

Eventually, they ended up walking onto a broad expanse of grass, pausing by a large central water fountain. "Where's the gunfire coming from?" Chance asked as the sound of bullets flying competed with the splattering of water.

"There's a target range to the east of us," Maria said. "When the clouds are low like they are today, the noise seems louder than usual, but you get used to it. It's the sound of freedom, after all."

"That's a good way to put it," he said. He gestured at a series of grassy mounds and then a row of what appeared to be bunkers against a hill, five of them in all. "What's all of that?"

"The mounds are a memorial for fallen patriots. The bunkers are used for storage now. Food, ammo, weapons, water, things like that. Originally they were intended as living quarters for new settlers. It was a time of high tension with Russia and they were intended to substitute as bomb shelters should the need arise. The big white house across the way there belongs to Richard Brighton. He lives with my sister and their—his—kids. My boys and I live in an extension near the back. It's a beautiful place." She checked her watch and added, "We better keep moving. My boys are out of school by now." As she led the way back to her car, she posed a question.

"What are your plans? Are you thinking of starting a small a business, for example? We could use a good mechanic."

"Not me," Chance said with a laugh. "I'm not the business type."

"Okay, well, then, for example, would you prefer a quiet neighborhood filled with children or a bigger parcel of land on which to raise crops or animals?"

"Children," he said quickly, determined to walk through any door she opened no matter how hard he had to squeeze through.

"Do you have any?" she asked.

"Not yet, but a man can dream. All I need to do is find my Dorrie."

"Then I'll drive you through one of the neighborhoods first."

"How many are there in all?"

"Three. They're all very pleasant."

It crossed his mind that he should ask a financial question or two. "How does the money part work?"

She smiled. "That's a discussion to be had with Mr. Brighton. Perhaps we can arrange a meeting for tomorrow.

"Mind if I ask why your store is outside the walls?"

"Not at all. It's a temporary location while I construct a new store one street over. See, my sister moved here years ago when she met and got involved with Robert Brighton. I used to visit her. I liked how uncomplicated things seemed. When my husband died a few years ago, I was left with two boys to raise. I thought what better place to do it than White Cliff." She drove under a small arch and added, "This is the first neighborhood."

The houses all looked relatively modest to Chance

while the land around them was utilized to the last degree. Dried cornstalks and pumpkins were about all that were left of the seasonal harvest, though some trees still held scattered apples and pears. Cords of firewood had been stacked against most of the fences. There were several windmills in evidence, used no doubt for power, and almost everyone had solar panels on their rooftops and propane tanks in their yards.

Several adults working outdoors and kids playing on the street added a comfortable ambience to the environment, but Chance's heart almost stopped beating when he spied a small blond boy sitting on a curb by himself. A second glance revealed it wasn't Charlie. He'd only just begun to recover from that disappointment when he glanced up to see a woman walking on the sidewalk in front of them. By the way she moved her head, it was obvious she was searching for someone or something.

"Stop!" Chance yelled and Maria instinctively applied the brakes. "It's a miracle," he said as he opened the door and ran after the woman. He hadn't seen her face but that shapeless gray sweater and the way she moved made it clear to him that he'd found Lily. His pounding footsteps must have alarmed her because when she turned, her eyes were huge.

"Chance! What are you doing—"

She didn't get a chance to finish because Chance grabbed her around the waist and hoisted her off the ground. He twirled her around, put her back down and bent his head to kiss her. It had been intended as a show of his enthusiasm to assure Maria he was an up-and-up guy, but the instant his lips touched Lily's, all bets were off. All the anxiety, anger, worry and pure raw emotion he'd been trying to tame for days raged inside his body as he claimed her.

She resisted for a half a heartbeat and then surrendered. She hadn't kissed him like this since the night out by the river. All the stories he'd told himself that one woman's kiss was much like another shot up in flames as he lost himself in the soft, moist oasis of her mouth. He blocked out everything but the sensation of having her to himself for what couldn't have been more than a couple of seconds but seemed to last forever.

But just as before, she broke the connection abruptly, breathlessly, though this time she didn't run away. Instead she looked up at him and slowly raised her hand to gently touch his cheek with her cold fingers. He felt the unexpected tender caress shoot through his body. "What are you doing here?" she whispered.

"What do you think I'm doing here?" He wrapped his hand around hers, trying to warm her. He finally remembered Maria and looked up as she pulled her car forward.

"Quick," he added. "There's not much time. You're my wife, my name is Pete Reed and you're Dorrie."

Maria exited her car and approached with a stately walk and a disapproving glance at Chance. "Lily, you know this man?"

"Yes," she said. "Pete is my husband."

"Lily? Is that what you're calling yourself?" Chance asked, staring into Lily's eyes, one of them still black and blue. He could almost see the imprint of Block's knuckles. "That was your mother's name," he added.

Lily touched Maria's arm. "I kind of thought Pete might show up. It's fine that he's here."

"You said *your husband* hit you," Maria said, her gaze

searching Lily's battered face before glancing again at Chance. "I don't like to pry, but she was in bad shape when she got here and we offered a temporary sanctuary."

"Now wait a second," he said, putting up his hands and backing away a step. "Dorrie knows I never hit her."

Lily smiled at him and then looked at Maria. "He didn't hit me," she mumbled.

"But you said your husband—"

"I said it wrong. What I meant was that after I left Pete, I went to my ex-husband's house to ask for money. He did this to me, not Pete."

Maria didn't look convinced. She'd been haughty the night before, friendly that day and now she looked suspicious. "Is there actually a warrant out for your arrest?"

"Yes. I didn't lie about that or Uncle Hank, either. I'm not ashamed of those things. May Pete stay in the apartment with me?"

"If that's your choice." Maria seemed to think for a second before speaking again. "The teacher you're subbing for needs help until the end of the week. That's three days. When she's ready to return, it would be best if you and Pete leave. If you've decided our community and way of life appeals to you, then submit an application. Mr. Brighton will review it and respond within ninety days. That's how it's done." She turned to Chance and added, "You can bring your truck inside the wall. Do you two want a ride back to Lily's, I mean Dorrie's apartment?"

"No, we'll walk," Lily said.

"Thanks for everything, Maria," Chance added.

"I better get back to work," was all she said.

They watched her drive away. A few children had gathered round them and Lily made it clear there could be no frank discussions in front of them. "Let's walk to the gate and get your truck," she said.

So holding hands like a reunited couple might, they walked the mile back to the gate so Chance could get his things out of the truck. Eventually, the kids petered out and they were alone. "Finally, we can talk," Lily said.

He put his arm around her shoulder to make sure they were close enough to speak in whispers as there were other people coming and going, most on foot as they were. "What were you doing walking around that neighborhood?" he asked. "And what did Maria mean when she said the teacher you're subbing for? And who's Uncle Hank?"

"I was searching the neighborhood for Charlie. As far as the teaching thing goes, I lucked into that. My class is full of ten-year-olds, but I managed to sneak down to the kindergarten room this morning. Charlie wasn't there. I don't even know if he's here."

"He's here," Chance said.

She turned her head and looked up at him. "He is? How do you know that for sure?"

"Because your husband sent me to get him back."

Her expression turned horrified. "You went to see Jeremy?"

"Yeah. Not right away. I had to get over being mad at you first."

She bit her lip. It was on the tip of his tongue to chastise her, but he held off.

"Jeremy actually said Charlie was here?"

"He seemed pretty damn sure. He told me Maria Eastern would know but warned me not to ask her outright."

"Maria? Well, she does seem enmeshed in things."

"She said today that she's here in White Cliff because her sister has a relationship with Robert Brighton."

"Really? What have you learned about Charlie from her?"

"Nothing. I wanted to ask her outright. I figured when she found out I wasn't working for Block she'd be open, but I didn't know what you had set up so I decided to wait to talk to you first."

"Maybe we should just go talk to her."

"I don't know," he said. "If she's responsible for taking Charlie then she's involved in kidnapping. If she knows who did take him, then she's an accessory after the fact. Either one of those charges are very serious. It seems unlikely she'd be chatty about it if she knows you're Charlie's mother and might bring charges."

"You know what's been bothering me? How did they even know Charlie was at Jeremy's house? He and I had been gone almost nine months."

"Maybe there's a neighbor someone paid off to report when and if Charlie returned."

"Or maybe Jeremy set this whole thing up to get rid of me forever," she said.

He squeezed her shoulder. "Okay, you'd better tell me what you told the people here so we don't trip each other up."

"I remembered a friend of my father's from a long time ago. He joined a cult down in Texas. There were rumors children were being abused. When the cult refused to submit to a government investigation and took up arms, there was a big invasion of sorts. My dad's friend was shot along with two kids and a policeman. In the way that can happen with these things, Dad's friend became a sort of legend. When I got here, I told them Hank Miller was my uncle. It was obvious his name was familiar to them. I said my husband had beat me up and I'd been on the run for a while. I asked for help."

Two men walking toward them scanned them uneasily. One was carrying an AK-47 slung over his back. Lily and Chance both smiled. They got zero response from the men who passed them by without saying a word. Chance hugged Lily closer to be able to whisper to her. "That must be why Block warned that police involvement with Charlie's kidnappers could be dangerous. He's afraid if law enforcement shows up, these people might defend their home turf and create a situation like the one down in Texas."

"But law enforcement showed up after Wallace Connor's death and asked about Fallon. Nothing terrible happened."

"They asked about someone who apparently doesn't exist. Coming to look for a kidnapped child is a whole different ball game."

"The key to this has to be Maria," Lily said. "We have to find out more about her. But who do we ask? I haven't spoken to a single person here but Maria, a couple of the teachers and a few kids. Everyone else just looks at me funny."

"Well, if we can't ask anyone in White Cliff, we'll have to ask elsewhere."

LILY SLID INTO the old red truck. She'd never seen it before, but having spent six months serving as a cook and housekeeper for the Hastings men, she knew there were barns and sheds aplenty with years of accumulated equipment tucked away here and there and everywhere. She doubted they even knew exactly how much stuff they had.

Instead of starting the truck, Chance sat with both hands on the steering wheel and stared through the windshield as if he was in a daze. She loved his strong profile and admired it for a bit, remembering the kiss of a few minutes before with a rush of pleasure. She could only imagine what it would be like to sleep with him, to have all his heat and power focused on her to the exclusion of anyone else. It was a very provocative concept.

He turned to face her and for a moment she wondered if her thoughts had somehow entered his consciousness.

"What are you thinking?" Lily asked.

"Neither Maria or her son, Dennis, knew anyone named Darke Fallon. They've all heard of him because the police came calling after the Connor shooting. Have you met Maria's other son?"

"No. I haven't even met Dennis. But Maria said her sons were less than a year apart in age."

"What I'm thinking is this. We've been concentrating on Fallon because he killed himself under your husband's watch, so to say. But the guy Fallon killed in that motel, he must have been someone's kid, too. If I'm remembering correctly, he was in his early twenties. I also remember he lived in Greenville and left a couple of family members behind. Greenville is roundabout six miles from here. I stayed there last night."

Lily had already started a search on her cell phone. "No one named Wallace Connor is listed but there is an O. Connor and there's also a place called Connor's Greenville Bakery, both in Greenville."

He glanced at his watch. "What time do they close the gate here?"

"Nine o'clock," Lily responded. "Are you suggesting we drive to Greenville?"

"Sure. We have plenty of time and we need to rule the Connor family out when it comes to taking Charlie."

"I know…but—"

"But what?"

She shook her head. "It feels wrong to leave here and drive into Greenville on a wild-goose chase. Charlie has to be behind one of these closed doors…"

"There are dozens and dozens of closed doors in White Cliff, Lily. Very few of them will actually open up to let you in."

"But there are more neighborhoods to search. I've only walked through two of them."

"Listen to yourself. You're looking for Charlie out in the open while all the houses sit up away from the road. He could be behind any one of the hundreds of windows and how would you know? This isn't the regular world where you can pretend to go door to door with a survey and look for him. These people are wary of strangers—"

"You think I don't know all of this?" she interrupted, her voice rising.

He took a deep breath. "Okay, I'll come with you and look through the other neighborhoods. There will still be time to hit Greenville when we finish with—"

"No, Chance, no. Two unknown adults walking side by side are intimidating to people. Remember the looks those men gave us? A lone woman just kind of disappears."

"Then I'll wait—"

"No, that's okay."

"But we should stay together."

She curled her fingernails against her palms. "This is the very reason I came alone," she said.

"Why?"

"I knew you'd try to micromanage me."

He took a deep breath before speaking carefully and she could hear the effort he put into holding his temper. "You're right. Charlie is your son and you didn't ask for me to come find you, in fact you went out of your way to make sure I didn't. But I'm here now, and I think we should take advantage of that. Since we can't walk the neighborhoods together, let's split up and cover twice the ground."

"I guess so," she said, getting out of the truck. "The next neighborhood isn't far, I'll walk." She shut the door louder than she had to.

She heard him start the engine as she walked stiffly toward the gate and then she stopped and turned. He hadn't moved the truck an inch. A debate raged inside her head. Some of what he said made sense. Instinct and love weren't always enough. Giving in to fear wasn't going to help. And what else had Jeremy told Chance that he hadn't yet shared that might help her figure this out?

She walked back to the truck, opened the passenger door and got inside. "I've decided we should drive into town," she said.

He didn't utter a word, just backed up the truck and headed out on the gravel road. Lily closed her eyes for a moment. Days of worry were taking their toll. She finally took a deep breath. "Chance? Are we going to talk?"

"About what?" he shot back as they finally hit pavement and turned toward Greenville. He didn't even glance at her as he asked.

"Listen, I'm sorry I seem ungrateful that you've come to help."

He spared her a quick glance. "I'm not here to undermine you, Lily. I'm only here because two heads are better than one. Charlie needs as many people on his side as he can get. And I knew that if I wasn't here helping I'd never know how this ended."

"What do you mean? I would have called you when this it's resolved."

"Really? Because with your track record, I was pretty sure I'd never hear from you again."

"My track record?"

"You're a quitter, Lily. You run away when things get scary."

She opened her mouth to refute his comment, but he interrupted her.

"You ran when I kissed you that first time. You ran when Jodie Brown came to the ranch. You ran when you decided I would be too much trouble to bring with you to White Cliff. And you want to run now."

"I didn't ask you to follow me here," she said.

"No, you didn't. You seldom ask anyone for much of anything. Is there a person in this world you trust?"

"Your father," she responded immediately.

"And yet even with him you didn't come clean and admit how serious your problems were with your husband. It's like you're afraid to give up any control at all."

She turned her head and stared out the passenger window. He thought he knew all about her! He thought he had her figured out. Couldn't he see it had taken her six years of a bloody, soul-draining marriage to finally grasp the raw edges of self-destiny? And now she was supposed to share it, to give it away?

"Maybe I do run when I feel threatened, but don't you think you do the same thing?" she said.

He looked perplexed. "What do you mean?"

"You're almost thirty-five years old. You've never had

a serious relationship. As soon as a woman starts to feel the slightest bit comfortable, poof, you're gone."

"That's not true," he said, but the shifting in his eyes revealed he wasn't so sure about it.

"Maybe we're more alike than you want to admit," she said.

He stared at her for a long moment before speaking again. "I never thought of myself as a quitter," he said. Was that pain in his eyes? Was it possible he'd actually considered what she said? He took a deep breath and added, "I guess when it comes to you I should have minded my own business right from the start. I don't know why I keep bugging you. But now it's about more than you and me, it's about Charlie. I like that kid. I want him to be safe, with you. Don't ask me to turn away from doing anything I can to make that happen." He cast her another wary glance. "Truce?"

"Truce."

Chapter Seven

"The bakery is straight down Main Street, left on Franklin," Lily said. She put the phone in her purse and added, "The residence is two blocks over on Lincoln."

"Let's start with the business," Chance said.

The bakery was in the middle of a block that looked as though nearby strip malls had exacted their toll on commerce. Parallel parking existed on either side of the two-way street that had been planted with numerous sugar maples. Their colorful leaves seemed to wage war against the increasingly gray skies, though defeat was inevitable.

There was a chill to the air that promised winter was soon to become a force to be reckoned with, and Chance saw Lily pull her sweater closer around her body and shiver.

The bakery itself was awash with pink. Pink walls, pink counter, pink trim. Most likely, he thought, the glass-fronted display cases would be filled with a decent variety of goodies in the morning. But this late in the afternoon, there were only a few loaves of bread and some tired-looking pastries to be had.

A girl who didn't look a day over sixteen stood behind the counter. Unsurprisingly, she wore a pink apron over her T-shirt and jeans. "Betsy" was embroidered in white over the pocket. Her face was round and lightly freckled, her eyes a pale blue. "Can I help you?" she asked, pausing in her chore of wiping fingerprints off a case door. There was a guarded look in her eyes.

"How about a loaf of bread?" Chance said.

"Wheat or whole grain. That's all we have left."

Chance looked at Lily who supplied the answer. "Whole grain. Boy, those pastries look good."

"They are," the girl said.

"Let's get the last three," Chance said. "Did you bake them?"

The girl shook her head causing the straight reddish-blond locks to slide across her shoulders. "No way. My dad gets up at three every morning and does the baking. He was depending on my brother to take over, but, well, anyway, Mom works here most of the day and then I come after school on Monday, Wednesday and Friday when I don't have band practice. Do you want the bread sliced?"

"That's okay, we'll do it ourselves," Lily said. "Is your dad or mom here now?"

"No. I'm closing the store today. You should try again tomorrow."

"We will," Chance said and then as though an afterthought had occurred, added, "Forgive me if this is a difficult question, but are you related to the man who was so senselessly killed last year down in Boise?"

Her eyes immediately filled with tears. "How did you know about Wallace?"

"I read about it in the paper. Are you his sister?"

"Yes," she said and flicked away a tear with shaky fingers.

"I'm sorry I brought it up," Chance said. "It must be terrible for you."

"That's an understatement," she said. "It just about destroyed my whole family."

"I know he had a girlfriend—" Lily began, but Betsy cut her off.

"Don't call her that! Tabitha Stevens is awful. Wallace was five years older than her and way out of her league but when Tabitha wants something, she's relentless and Wallace was as stupid as the next guy when it came to girls like her."

She took a deep breath as though winded and shook her head. Her face had turned red and blotchy. "She killed him, not that hitchhiker. Oh, I mean that Fallon guy obviously turned Wallace's knife on him and stabbed him, I mean, he confessed and everything, but I just know Tabitha pushed Wallace into taking that stupid trip. And then she walked around town boohooing like she's Juliet and she's lost her Romeo. It made me sick."

"What did the police—"

"The police? Don't make me laugh. That girl can cry like a banshee. They all fell for her lies. Everyone in this town thinks she's a poor little thing because her boyfriend got killed. Wallace was my brother. My family is the one who lost someone they loved, not Tabitha."

Chance glanced down at Lily who was staring in wide-eyed wonder at Betsy. "I'm really sorry we brought it up," Lily said to the girl. "You're obviously still in a lot of pain. But it will get better. I know people always say that but it's because it's true."

"I don't want it to get better," she said. "I want to hate Tabitha forever. If I can ever prove to the town what she really is, that'll be the day I'll finally feel better."

"What do you mean what she really is?" Lily asked.

"She was running around on Wallace."

"With who?"

"I don't know who. I heard rumors. I still hear rumors. And about two weeks ago I was coming home from a band concert and I saw Tabitha sneaking around over by the east side of town. It's dark and dangerous over there and she was alone and it was late. I tell you, she's rotten to the bone." She stopped speaking and took a deep breath as though to center herself. "I know I sound terrible," she added.

"You just sound angry," Lily said gently. "It's how you feel."

"Yeah," she said, slipping the pastries into the bag with the bread. "You owe me eight dollars and fifty-five cents."

"Something else," Lily said as Chance paid for the goods. "Do you have much to do with the people up at White Cliff?"

"Not too much," Betsy said. "They come into town now and again but they make people nervous and don't ever say too much unless you get them started and then they go on and on about politics."

"Do you know any of them, I mean personally?"

"Not really. There was one lady a year or two ago who was nice. I guess she runs a store up there. She and her sons used to come to town now and again and she was kind of friendly. Her oldest boy is cute."

"You're talking about Maria," Lily said.

"Yeah, do you know her?"

"We're staying up that way for a couple of days and she's been like the White Cliff ambassador of sorts."

"Yeah. Well, some of those people have been up there for years and they've gotten kind of standoffish. Maria was different."

"Was?"

Betsy shrugged. "I haven't seen her in a long time but the last time she came in here to buy bread, she was different. Kind of quiet and preoccupied, I guess. She didn't smile and she always used to smile."

"When did she change?"

Betsy narrowed her eyes in concentration. "A while ago. After Christmas sometime." She handed them the bag. Lily reached for it right as the bell on the door announced another customer. A boy about Betsy's age seemed surprised she wasn't alone.

"Hey, Todd," Betsy said.

"Hey," he responded. He ran a finger along the glass case. He reminded Chance of himself about that age, still growing into the man he'd become with time. His shoulders and buzz-cut hair glistened with water. Chance glanced through the window to see the clouds had finally broken.

"Do you want something?" Betsy asked. Her voice had undergone a distinct change from impatient to silky.

"No, just hanging out," he said and flashed her a smile. His voice cracked as he added, "I thought you'd be alone."

Betsy cast Lily and Chance a pleading look.

"We're just leaving," Lily said, and they beat a hasty retreat.

"Whew," Lily said as they stood on the sidewalk under the awning. "That poor girl is a walking, breathing emotional roller coaster."

"She hates Tabitha and apparently has a thing for Todd," Chance agreed. "I can't see how either of those concern us, but the news about Maria changing is interesting."

"It's gotten cold," Lily said, stretching the poor sweater even tighter around her body.

Chance looked at the stores lining the other side of the

street and added, "Follow me," grabbed her hand and led her across two lanes of sparse traffic.

The store they entered wasn't the kind Chance was used to navigating. Mannequins on one wall modeled what he guessed was the latest in fashion while circular racks held dozens of slacks, dresses and sweaters. The saleswoman hastened their way and asked how she could help them. "This lady needs a warm coat and a sweater and whatever else she wants," he said.

"Come this way," the saleswoman coaxed Lily as she moved toward the back of the store.

"We don't have time for this," Lily protested.

"Then don't waste what time we do have arguing," he said.

"I don't want you buying me clothes," she added stubbornly.

"I'm not. I'm using your husband's money. Technically, I guess it's more your money than mine as I lied to get it."

"Money he gave you to find Charlie?"

"More or less."

The furrowing of her brow suggested she would ask him more about this later. "Okay, I'll get a coat, but don't keep calling that man my husband."

He shrugged.

Fifteen hurried minutes later, they left the store four hundred dollars poorer but at least Lily looked warm in her new faux fur lined raincoat. She carried three shopping bags as well, full of everything from warm pajamas to jeans and walking shoes. She hadn't tried on a single garment, just bought them off the rack, so distracted by the clock that Chance wasn't sure she even knew what she'd chosen.

"I asked the saleswoman about Maria and White Cliff," she said as they got back in the truck. "She had no idea who I was talking about. I gather this is her first winter this far north and the rain is already getting to her."

The Connor house was a modest one-story affair built of brick. Nobody's yard looked great this time of year and theirs was no exception. The rain was quickly turning the sparse grass brown with mud, the cracked cement walkway was slippery with moss as though the front entry was seldom used. They made their way carefully to the front door and knocked.

It took a few minutes, but eventually the door opened and a faded-looking woman of about forty faced them. "May I help you?"

"We wondered if we could talk to you and your husband for a few minutes," Chance asked politely.

"What about?" she asked.

"Your son, Wallace."

"What about my son?" she said, her voice shaking now. "He's dead and gone, murdered for a measly two hundred dollars and a ring. They didn't even take his credit cards. What can you possibly want to talk to us about?"

"Darke Fallon."

A man showed up behind the woman. He appeared to be ten or so years older than her, a smallish guy with a lightly freckled round face and graying hair. Light blue eyes peered from behind wire-framed glasses. "Let them in, Carolyn," he said.

The woman opened the door wider and Chance followed Lily over the threshold. The room they entered was sparsely furnished but fastidiously clean. The woman motioned at the sofa and asked if they'd like anything hot to drink. They declined. The house smelled great to Chance, like roast beef, like home. The table in the corner had been set for dinner.

"My name is Otto," he said, "and this is my wife, Carolyn. Now what's this about our Wallace?"

Chance introduced himself and Lily who immediately asked if she could use their restroom. Carolyn pointed out the way and Lily left the room.

"First of all, I should mention that we stopped at your bakery and talked to Betsy," Chance said.

"About Wallace?" Otto said with a quick glance at his wife.

"Yes."

"Did she cry much?" Otto asked.

"A little. She also talked about Wallace's girlfriend, Tabitha."

"Uh-oh," Carolyn said. She'd perched on the edge of a chair and now folded her hands together between her knees. "Betsy gets kind of wound up when it comes to Tabitha."

"There's no love lost between them," Otto agreed.

"What do you think of Tabitha?"

"She's just a kid," Otto said. "Works a shift at the Burger Barn south of town, seems popular. Comes from a dysfunctional family but just about everyone seems to these days. We didn't see too much of her. Wallace lived with a friend across town and seldom brought Tabitha to our house. I think he was kind of embarrassed because she was his little sister's age."

"And the girls didn't like each other," Carolyn added. "But Betsy shouldn't be bad-mouthing her to strangers. By all accounts, Tabitha was in terrible shape after Wallace's funeral. My heart went out to the girl."

Otto cleared his throat. "You said you wanted to talk about the man who killed Wallace. You do realize no one knows much about him?"

"No one knows anything about him," Carolyn said.

"I read a sketchy article about the murder," Chance explained. "I can hardly believe the police couldn't identify Fallon."

"I know," Otto said. "Neither could we. He said he was hitchhiking from Bend, Oregon, where he lived, but there was no evidence a guy by that name ever lived there. Fallon isn't an unusual last name but the Darke part is different. Anyway, when asked about his friends, the only names he gave were first names like Johnny or Dave or Nick. He said he used Wallace's hunting knife to rob him and when Wallace refused to hand over his money, he stabbed him. But the kid was not only younger than Wallace, he was about half his size. And then the police said it appeared he'd been stabbed while lying down, not standing. But then again, the boy did have Wallace's blood on him."

"How did the police explain the stabbing position discrepancy?"

"They really couldn't. One of the officers told us that Fallon must have lied about what happened. It makes more sense that Fallon came into Wallace's room after he was asleep and killed and robbed him and just didn't want to admit it. Wallace had been drinking that night. His blood alcohol numbers were high."

"He could sleep pretty soundly after a six-pack of beer," Carolyn added.

"What about the murder weapon?" Chance asked.

"Wallace's own knife. It was still in the van when they caught Fallon. He'd tried to wipe it clean, but there were traces of blood on the blade. It was a hunting knife Wallace carried with him all the time."

"He wore it where people could see it?"

"Not really, but for all we know, he'd taken it off when he drove and that's when Fallon saw it. Who knows what they talked about in that van? Wallace was a friendly guy."

"You mentioned a ring," Chance said.

"Yeah. It had a nice stone in it but it wasn't worth more than a few hundred dollars and that was because of the gold. Fallon said he lost it in a river when he stopped to wash all the blood off his clothes. He didn't know which river and he didn't get all of it."

"And he left a bloody footprint in Wallace's room," Carolyn added. "The police said he seemed a little slow-witted. He stopped talking when the questions got tricky. Didn't say a word after that first confession, apparently not even to his court-appointed attorney. And why did he drive around all that time in Wallace's truck?"

"Yeah," Otto said. "And why was Wallace down in Boise to begin with?"

"The newspaper said he was there for a job interview, didn't they?" Chance asked with a glance toward the hallway Lily had disappeared down several minutes ago. What was taking her so long?

"Bah," Otto said. "He worked at the bakery with me. In a few years it would have been his. They couldn't find a single employer down there who admitted setting up an interview with him. All they had to go on was his roommate's word that that's where Wallace said he was going."

"And Tabitha called us and the roommate the next morning to ask about Wallace because he hadn't shown up for a date the night before. If he was going on a job interview, wouldn't he have told her?"

Lily appeared just then and sat down next to Chance right as Otto posed another question. "Why are you asking about Fallon? Do you think you know who he was?"

"No," Chance said. "But do you think it's possible he lived at White Cliff?"

Otto looked at Carolyn again. "I doubt it," she finally said. "The boy had no papers on him, no fingerprints matched up anywhere. Nothing. The police talked to everyone here and everyone up there and no one knew a thing about a Darke Fallon. No one from there was missing, just like no one here was unaccounted for. This Fallon must have been a drifter, maybe from another country or something. I don't know."

"Why do you care where he came from?" Otto asked. "And why are you asking so many questions about Wallace's murder?"

Lily answered this time. "I have a five-year-old boy," she said. "His name is Charlie and we have reason to suspect that the Fallon family might have taken him. We want to talk to them. I need to get my son back—"

She stopped speaking as her voice choked. Chance put his arm around her shoulders. "If you guys think of anything that might help, please let us know," he said. "We're actually staying at White Cliff in a guest apartment."

"I didn't know they let outsiders in," Otto said.

"That reminds me," Chance added. "Do you know a woman named Maria Eastern? Your daughter said she used to come into your bakery."

"Don't recognize the name," Otto said. "How about you, Carolyn?"

"No. Betsy is a lot better with names than I am, though. Is she important?"

"Who knows?" Chance said. He gave them his cell number and Lily's, too. "Please call if you think of anything."

"What about the police?" Carolyn asked. "What are they doing about this?"

"There are complicated reasons they haven't been called yet," Lily said.

"Can't say as they got very far in our case, but they tried," Otto commented.

Chance and Lily thanked them for their time. Their last glimpse of the couple was as Carolyn closed the door and switched on the porch light.

LILY SHIVERED INSIDE her new coat as they walked back to the truck.

"What took you so long in the bathroom?" Chance asked her.

"I wasn't in the bathroom, I was searching the house for some sign a small boy was being held there. That's why we went, right? To see if they might be involved in Charlie's abduction?"

"Right. But I'd bet money those people would rather cut off their arms than put another person through what they've endured."

"I get the same feeling," she said. "And besides that, I didn't find anything to suggest Charlie has ever been in that house."

He opened her door and she climbed in. The stress and disappointment of the past hour had caused a horrible headache and she closed her eyes. All she could see was Carolyn's face, the sadness and loss in her eyes.

The woman would never see her son again. Did a similar fate await Lily?

She was determined not to cry, not to make a scene, not to be weak, but her heart felt broken and she didn't know if it would ever mend. As the rain pelted the truck's windshield, she buried her face in her hands and wept.

Chance pulled the truck off to the side of the road and gathered her into his arms. She was crying so hard by then it was difficult to get a breath, impossible to talk and he held her for what seemed an hour, rocking her gently, smoothing her hair, his body big and warm and comforting. She could get used to being treated with such gentleness. She felt small and treasured in his embrace, a feeling she hadn't experienced since her mother died when she was six. Her father had climbed too deep inside a gin bottle to worry much about parenting.

The sobs abated and she took a few deep breaths. Anxious to look anywhere but in his eyes, she glanced out the window. "Where are we?" she asked as she dug a packet of tissues from her purse.

"I was going to go to a place called the Burger Barn," Chance said. "I'll go tomorrow. Right now, it's time to get you back to White Cliff."

"Are you hungry?" she asked as she blew her nose.

"Now that you mention it, yes, but that wasn't why I wanted to hit the place. Otto says that Tabitha Stevens works there. I hoped she might be pulling an evening shift."

"Why bother with her?" Lily said. "What can she possibly tell us that would help find Charlie?"

"I don't know," he said, scooting back across the bench seat to his place behind the wheel. "But she may know something about Darke Fallon or Maria Eastern that she didn't tell the police, or maybe she's since remembered something. I thought it was worth ruling her out."

"Because of what Betsy said about Tabitha having other boyfriends?"

"Partially. I guess I'm a turn-every-stone kind of guy. But I can do this on my own. It's been a tough afternoon and—"

"Let's go now," Lily said. "I want to see if this kid is the trollop Betsy made her out to be. Besides, it's dark and I can't think of anything we can do at White Cliff to get closer to finding Charlie so we might as well check out Tabitha. Do you know where this place is?"

"Not really. I was going to have you check your phone, but you looked terrible after we left the Connors'."

"I'm better now," she said, wiping away the last of the tears. "The look in Carolyn's eyes just got to me."

He smiled at her. "You know, your face is beginning to heal. You're almost pretty again."

She laughed out loud and hit his arm. "I'll look up the Burger Barn."

A few minutes later, they pulled in front of a fast food place that appeared to have been built in the fifties. They went inside and found a seat where they could see the whole restaurant.

The wait staff all wore blue jeans and red checkered shirts and all seemed to be teenagers except for one woman in her forties who had to feel like a babysitter with these kids. The place was crammed, and music blared from a Wurlitzer jukebox. After the emptiness of the town, the bustling activity in the little diner was amazing.

The older waitress brought them ice water and asked

if they wanted a menu. Chance asked what the specialty was and she looked at him like he was nuts. "Burgers."

"What's the best one?" he said.

"Folks seem to really enjoy the bacon cheese burger."

"Then that's what I'll have. Add fries and a chocolate shake. How about you, Lily?"

"The same," she said because it was easier than thinking about it.

The waitress hustled off and they took turns studying the other staff. There looked to be two beefy guys working the kitchen behind the window and four females and two males taking orders and delivering food. The girls all looked about Betsy's age. One had very long red hair she wore in a high ponytail that she whipped around like a horse's tail on a hot fly-infested afternoon. Another girl was a slender blonde who bit her fingernails when she thought no one was watching, and the last two had dark hair, one cut short, another shoulder length, both kind of nondescript. They all moved about the restaurant and back into the kitchen with quick, sure steps. The operation looked efficient, friendly and unremarkable.

Their food arrived a lot faster than Lily had thought it would. The waitress asked what else they wanted. Chance said nothing but Lily lowered her voice. "Is Tabitha Stevens working here tonight?"

"Why do you want to know? Did she sass you or something? If she did, don't tell her grandfather, okay?"

"Her grandfather?"

"Pastor Stevens. At least he used to be a preacher. Anyway, he's real strict. Tabitha is a handful but I hate to see her in trouble and it isn't because I have a kind heart, she just acts out her hostility and the customers complain and then the manager calls her grandfather and things get worse. She's been real moody lately anyway."

"Don't worry," Lily said quickly. "She didn't do anything. I just know her mother and since I was traveling through this way, thought I'd say hello to Tabitha. I heard she worked here."

"Tabitha's mother has been dead three years," the woman said. "Her grandpa raises her now."

"I know," Lily said, scrambling to think of some excuse for wording her comment in the present tense, but she shouldn't have worried. Another table demanded attention and the waitress left to comply.

"You're a lousy liar," Chance said.

"I know."

He took a bite of his hamburger and made a contented sound in his throat. Lily looked down at the food and started to push it away, but took a French fry instead. Eating hadn't exactly been a priority lately but that fry tasted like greasy ambrosia and she ate another. Then she tried the hamburger. By the time she slurped down the last of the milkshake, her headache had disappeared and she felt ready to track down her missing son. She would find Charlie tomorrow, come hell or high water. They were running out of time in White Cliff and for some reason she couldn't pin down, she wasn't anxious to meet Robert Brighton, the man behind the place.

"Nice to see you eat a meal," Chance said.

"I was hungrier than I thought."

He leaned toward her. "I've been meaning to ask you something," he said as he lowered his voice. "Have you seen any sign of McCord in White Cliff?"

"McCord? You mean that guy who works for Jeremy? No, of course not. Why would he be up here?"

He started to answer when the waitress with the red hair showed up at their table. Gone was the ponytail. Her hair now hung loose on her shoulders, completely covering one eye in an old Veronica Lake look that appeared way too sophisticated for a teen in Greenville, Idaho. She'd also undone a couple of buttons, revealing an eyeful of cleavage, and knotted her blouse above the waistband of skintight jeans. The tennis shoes all the waiters wore had been exchanged for pointy red heels and she'd applied makeup with a heavy hand. The expression in her dark-rimmed eyes was calculating, her stance challenging. "I heard you were asking about me," she said, directing her comment to Chance.

So this was Tabitha Stevens. "Yes, we were," Lily said. "Would you like to sit down for a minute?"

"I wouldn't mind," the girl said. "My shift is just about over anyway."

Before Lily could move her coat and purse to make room, the girl claimed the scant twelve inches on Chance's side of the booth. He slid along to make more room for her but she seemed to ooze along with him.

Her behavior with Chance struck Lily as surprisingly brazen. There was no doubt he'd been endowed with his share of the Hastings male charm and good looks and often affected women with a certain rakish gleam in his eye; it just seemed odd this girl would feel so comfortable with a stranger twice her age.

Tabitha tore her gaze from Chance and stared at Lily. "Why were you asking about me? How did you know my mother?"

Lily saw Chance's lips twitch, probably because he was anticipating how she would dig herself out of this hole. "I didn't know your mother," Lily said. "We just wanted to ask you a few questions."

"So, ask."

"We were hoping you could tell us something about Wallace Connor."

Tears seemed to shoot into Tabitha's eyes. "Poor Wally," she lamented. "I don't know if I can bear to talk about him. I was sick for weeks after that maniac stabbed him to death."

"It must have been horrible for you."

"How about Darke Fallon?" Chance ventured.

Tabitha groaned. "Not *him* again. I told the police I never met anyone named Darke Fallon. What kind of name is that, anyway? I'm sick of hearing about him. He murdered Wally. Let him burn in hell."

"We weren't actually planning a rescue party to the underworld," Chance commented.

Tabitha turned to look up at him, the unshed tears making her eyes look huge and innocent. She smiled and said, "That's funny."

"We'd just like to talk to the Fallon family," Lily said.

"You and everyone else. I can't help you. As far as I know, he was just one of those homeless, nameless freaks that ruin other people's lives."

"How about a woman named Maria Eastern?"

Tabitha tilted her head to the side as though thinking. "No," she said. "Who is she?"

"She owns a store right outside White Cliff."

"Those freaks!" she said. "Why would I know someone like that? Hey, wait, are you one of them?"

"No," Chance said. "We've only known Maria for a day or two. We're staying up at White Cliff. I know she has a son about your age, so we just wondered if you'd met her."

"A son? What's his name?"

"Dennis," Chance said.

"There's another son named Jacob," Lily added.

Tabitha shook her head. "Never heard of either of them. Those kids don't go to our schools and we don't go to theirs." She drummed acid-green fingernails on the tabletop. "Is that all you want to know?" When Chance nodded, she slid out of the booth, started to walk away and turned. The tears were gone and the look she cast Lily was concentrated venom. "I think it was cruel of you to even ask me about Wally. You're as bad as Betsy."

"His sister?"

"Betsy the bitch," she said. "She's always coming in here. She sits in my section and glares at me. I'm the only one who loved Wally and she is stupid and ugly and mean." With that she stalked off.

Chance put enough money on the table to cover the bill and a tip, and they got to their feet. Sitting near the door at a table they hadn't noticed before, they found Betsy sipping on a cola. "I told you she was awful," she said as they passed.

Chapter Eight

When they went outside, they found the rain had let up, though the moon did little to penetrate the still hovering clouds. "Time to get back to White Cliff," Chance said with little enthusiasm as he found the place oppressive.

How did little Charlie feel about it?

He helped Lily into the truck and for a few minutes, they just sat there. He could feel the energy drain from Lily and touched her arm to urge her across the seat and closer to him. With his arm around her shoulders, he whispered against her cool, silky hair. "You're exhausted," he said.

She turned and looked up at him. They were parked in a dark corner of the lot so there wasn't much of her to see except the whites of her eyes and the glimmering ivory of her coat. "I'm not so much tired as discouraged," she said. "But I've made a decision. I'm going to show up at the school tomorrow and talk to the kindergarten people, then I'm going to go find Robert Brighton and level with him. If he kicks me out of there, then I'm calling the police. It's been three days now since Charlie was taken and I'm no closer to finding him than I ever was. I don't care what Jeremy says, something has to be done."

"I don't blame you," Chance said, "but I suggest we

start with Maria. She already kind of knows us and maybe as a woman and a mother, she'll be easier for you to reason with."

"I'll think about it," she said. He felt her fingers touch his face, and he sighed.

"I'm sorry I called you a quitter. It's really not true," he said.

"Yes, it is," Lily murmured. "But my reasons for running have always made sense to me. I don't know, I guess I'm just so scared all the time."

"Are you scared now?"

"For Charlie, of course."

"Are you scared of me, Lily?"

She nuzzled his neck. "I'm scared of what you represent to me."

"And what's that?" he asked, kissing her ear and then her cheekbone.

"Security," she said. "Eternity. Big old concepts that seem to unilaterally unhinge men."

"Not all men," he said, bestowing soft kisses on her eyelids.

"I'm afraid of wanting what I won't be able to have," she said, and before he could respond, guided his lips to her own. The kiss lingered, tender and almost shy at first, but gaining momentum as the seconds slipped by. His fingers lay across her throat and he could feel the pounding of her heart. It was intoxicating to taste her, absorb her. If he'd been sixteen, he would have tried to strip off her clothes and make love to her in the front seat, but those days required a recklessness he no longer possessed. Besides, one way or another, he was going to make her his if only for one night and that night was not going to take place in a truck.

Still, when her hands crept up under his shirt, he shivered deep inside. His fingers roamed her body as well, sure she would put him off as he undid the clasp on her front-closing bra but she didn't. Her freed breasts felt gloriously warm and soft, and the tight, excited nubs of her nipples made his hunger for her jump off the charts.

His head kept screaming, *Stop or lose it right here, right now*, until the warning finally fought its way upstream through a tidal wave of hormones. She seemed to have been struggling with the same war of need versus poor planning. The kisses began to taper, grew gentle again, hands avoided decidedly sensitive areas and his erection throbbed with disappointment.

They finally separated and took deep breaths. "Wow, Chance," she said. "That was some kiss. I can see why all the town girls follow you around."

"It's a gift," he said, lowering his head to kiss her neck.

She laughed softly. "I know I'm sending you mixed messages," she whispered.

"Sort of."

He could hear her readjusting her clothes. "I'm sorry about that," she said.

"You don't need to be sorry, Lily."

"You just seem to be the epicenter of my crisscrossed desires."

"I'll take that…for now," he said. "But I'm warning you the next time we take it that far and don't finish it my head is going to explode."

"Okay," she said softly.

"Because it's surely no surprise that I find you irresistible."

"I thought you found me annoying," she whispered.

"I do. That's part of your irresistibility." He leaned

forward and kissed her again, then straightened up. "Time to go or we're going to get locked out of White Cliff." He reached for the keys and noticed how thoroughly they'd managed to fog up the windows. He ran his hand against the cold, wet glass, causing a sparkly river of condensation to cascade down the glass. Beside him, Lily breathed in quickly. "Look," she said as she peered past his head. He turned to see what had caught her attention.

"Over there, walking down the street."

"Is that Tabitha?"

"Yes. Look at the wobbly way she moves in those high heels."

"She must be freezing," Chase said as the girl passed beneath a street lamp. She'd topped her jeans and knotted shirt with a lacy, flimsy shawl that billowed out behind her. "I wonder where she's headed."

"She's on her way to meet someone," Lily said. "Dressed like that, I'd wager it's a guy." Tabitha left the lamplight and Chase was about to look away when another figure passed under the light, this one stealthily.

"That's Betsy," he said softly as though she might hear him. "She's following Tabitha." He turned to Lily. "Are you game?"

"Why not?"

They quickly got out of the truck using one door and locking it behind them. The last thing Chance wanted was for someone to steal his truck, and with it, his guns.

They walked quietly up the slight incline to the sidewalk on which they'd seen the girls. Chance wasn't sure why Lily was willing to follow them—he wasn't even sure why he wanted to. Curiosity? Partially. But it also had to do with Carolyn and Otto Connor and their loss.

Betsy was their only child now and she was sneaking around following Tabitha on a dark, overcast night.

They could no longer see Tabitha, but they could catch glimpses of Betsy and by the covert way she was moving, it was obvious she was still on Tabitha's trail. Many of the houses along the way had put Halloween decorations out on their lawns so they had to dodge the lights cast across the grass. And then there were the occasional cars whose headlights swept over them as they moved. Chance thought that an aerial picture of Betsy following Tabitha and them following Betsy would be worth a chuckle to an onlooker.

Chance estimated they'd walked a dozen blocks when they lost sight of Betsy. A car came along and illuminated the sidewalk up ahead for a moment but there was no sign of her. After the vehicle passed, they saw the girl emerge from the shelter of a parked car and resume walking. They followed. She crossed the street and they claimed a hiding place behind a large tree. They waited a few seconds before carefully peeking out to see what Betsy was up to.

She stood on the opposite sidewalk staring at a dark building situated on a large, partially overgrown corner lot. A steeple rose into the night sky. Chance realized it was an old church, but judging from the boards across some of the windows and a general feeling of neglect, it wasn't used as such anymore.

Betsy stared for a few more seconds, then she seemed to shake her head. She turned and they realized she was coming back their way. Standing very still, their hopes were simple: that she would stay on that side of the street and that a car wouldn't come by to expose them. She was walking faster now that she wasn't trailing anyone and eventually disappeared from view.

Chance and Lily cautiously crossed the street. "This is the east side of town," Chance said. "Remember Betsy told us she saw Tabitha over this way before?"

"Yes. But why was she following her?"

"Who knows?" Chance said, his gaze on the hulking building in front of them. "Maybe she was as curious as we were."

"I have a flashlight on my key chain," Lily said as she dug it from her handbag. It emitted a tiny little stream of weak light but it was marginally better than nothing. "Let's see if we can figure out where Tabitha went and what she's up to."

They climbed the church stairs but found the door boarded and locked. When they reached ground level again, Lily's flashlight revealed an overgrown path leading around to the back of the church. As it had rained earlier, it was impossible to tell if anyone had used it until Lily pointed at a couple of muddy footprints, each with a corresponding puncture like a high heel would make.

They practically tiptoed along the path that ran behind the church and beside an iron fence. The fence appeared to surround an old graveyard. Most of the tombstones were weathered and tilting. Once past the gate leading into the graveyard, the path came to a circular area that must have once been a garden. Leading off that was another stairway, this time to a back door. Boards stacked beside the door might once have been nailed across the opening to discourage access, but they'd been taken off. The knob turned easily in Chance's hand and when Lily's flashlight picked up traces of mud inside the building, they knew Tabitha was in the church somewhere.

The room they entered was empty. It led into a much larger space where old pews were still lined up in two rows on either side of an open aisle. The pulpit stood at the front, but little else remained. A tiny bit of outside light made it through the cracks between the boards.

One side of this room had several open doors leading from it and they checked out each in turn, disturbing dust at times. Near the front, they found a closed door and listened with ears against the wood for a few seconds to make sure they couldn't hear voices on the other side. At last they opened the door and found themselves at the head of a rickety-looking stairway leading down.

Chance took the flashlight from Lily. "I'll go first."

She rested her hand atop his shoulder and he actually smiled to himself. Unable to resist the temptation, he turned around and kissed her briefly and wondered how and when they'd managed to get to the point where he could do that without her slugging him or running off.

The stairs were sturdier than they looked and descended to a small cement area that held nothing other than what appeared to be a couple of old wooden panels that had been deposited against the wall. Another closed door stood directly in front of them and from the room beyond came the sound of two voices, a male and a female. Chance handed Lily the flashlight so he could investigate the panels. She immediately turned off her light and just in time, because the door suddenly rattled. Chance pulled her under cover of the wooden panels right as the door opened. The tight quarters prevented them from seeing anything, but they could hear every word and it was Tabitha's voice that dominated.

"You creep," she said. She obviously held a better light source as the room was brighter than it had been. "How could you, and with *her* of all people!"

The responding male voice sounded young, too. "Don't be like that, Tabby," he said and his voice cracked. Chance felt Lily jerk as she heard it, too. "Come here, come on, kiss me."

"Don't call me Tabby. I'm not a freaking cat."

"No, you're just a freaking freak!"

The unmistakable sound of a slap was followed by a mumbled oath and then hurried footsteps as one of them ran up the stairs. It must have been Tabitha because the boy swore again and raced after her.

"That was Todd," Lily whispered.

"The plot thickens," Chance responded.

LILY SHONE THE little flashlight around the room they entered. A big furnace that looked as though it hadn't warmed so much as a mouse in decades squatted in one corner. What appeared to be a workbench ran along another wall, its sole adornment an inexpensive-looking CD player and a few empty beer bottles. Tucked in a corner, they found a cot topped with a couple of rumpled blankets and a pillow. Another closed door finished off the decor and Chance opened that to reveal a small stack of used bricks, a broom and a spool of some kind of wire. Shelves on the back wall were surprisingly cluttered with odds and ends.

"This must have been the maintenance room," Chance said.

"Now a teenage love nest," Lily said. "Is that why

Betsy trailed Tabitha, because she either knew or was suspicious about a relationship her boyfriend had with Tabitha?"

"Why else?" Chance said.

"Her brother..."

"Died months and months ago at the hand of a mysterious man who confessed his guilt. Maybe Betsy feels as though Tabitha has already taken too much from her."

Lily nodded as she turned the light back into the room and focused on the cot. On the wall behind it, someone had carved initials. T.S. and W.C. and encircled it with a heart. A black line had been drawn to cross it out. Tabitha Stevens and Wallace Connor? Maybe. Lily hoped Wallace's parents never saw this tawdry place. There was another heart next to it that appeared to have been created using the same black ink as the line that crossed out the first heart. This time the initials T.S. and J.B. were crudely drawn.

Was this like a trophy bed for Tabitha? It seemed strange a girl would do something like this and yet there was no doubting that Tabitha was a young woman with an attitude and an appetite.

A glimpse of pale lace caught Lily's attention and she took a few steps to get closer. What was that crunching sound? As she looked down at the floor, she heard footsteps and instantly turned off the flashlight, grabbed Chance's arm and pushed him into the closet, closing the door quietly behind them,

He apparently hadn't heard the footsteps and started to speak, but she put a finger where she assumed his mouth was to hush him. His lips were soft, his breath warm and she was distracted for a second until a band of light streamed through the gap under the closet door.

Todd swore under his breath. "First she hits me and then she sends me on an errand," he mumbled. "Where is that thing? Oh." The door slammed a second later and the closet once again plunged into darkness.

"Tabitha left her shawl on the bed," Lily whispered. She started to move and tripped on the spool of wire. Afraid a crash would bring Todd running back, she grabbed the shelves for support. To her surprise, the whole wall kind of rocked beneath her hand. "Chance?" she whispered.

"I'm right here."

"The back wall moves."

"You mean the shelves are wobbly?"

"No, the whole thing feels like it could rotate or something." She turned on the flashlight whose beam was visibly weaker than it had been.

Chance put his hands on the shelves and wiggled them. They could both see and feel movement. He took the light from Lily and shined it on the unit. "You know, these shelves don't look as old as the church. And they're screwed in instead of nailed. Someone retrofitted this unit."

Lily tugged on one of the cans. "It's stuck," she said.

Chance gripped another and when it refused to budge, another. "They're all stuck. That's too big a coincidence. They must have been glued in place."

"Chance, maybe these shelves are really a secret door. In the movies there's always a candlestick or a book that acts as a lever."

They both immediately started pulling on various items. Chance hit the jackpot a few moments later when he touched a red vinyl binder with "maintenance schedule" written on the spine. He tilted it toward himself, and they could both see the hinge at the base of the binder that activated a mechanism. The shelving unit twisted silently in the middle creating space on either side.

"Well, I'll be," Chance said.

Lily shined her flashlight around. The floor and walls were all made of dirt reinforced with lumber. Best of all, a lantern hung on a hook to the left. As Chance lifted it free and switched it on, Lily turned off her flashlight.

"It's a tunnel," she said.

"It's a scary-looking thing," Chance added. "That wood looks like it's one day away from collapsing under the weight of all that dirt above it." Ground water had also seeped from the earth. The place had a forbidding, dank appearance and feel.

"Do you think Tabitha or Todd know about this?"

He shined the lantern light on the ground. "I can see a few footprints dried in the mud. Hard to tell when they were made," he said. "There's no way to know for sure, but I'd wager they don't have the slightest idea this is here. Let's take a look." He touched a more obvious lever next to the hook that had held the lantern and the door swung closed without a squeak.

It was only wide enough to walk single file. Chance led the way. Lily followed along, but as the tunnel kept going and going, she began to get anxious. The oppressive smell of the earth along with the occasional previous collapses jarred already frazzled nerves. But more important than that, how was investigating this tunnel helping them find Charlie?

They finally came to a wide spot of sorts. A metal trunk sat against the wooden support and Lily stopped walking. "Look at that," she said. "What's it doing here?"

"Someone had to bring it for some reason," Chance said and then chuckled. "Do I sound like Captain Obvious?"

She smiled. "It's not very big, but I have to sit down for a minute or two and it'll do." The day had held so many levels of stress that it seemed to have lasted forever. The trunk provided an adequate perch. Chance set the lantern on the floor and sat beside her. Lily leaned her head against his shoulder and peered up ahead where the tunnel stretched on into darkness. The silence felt tangible and when she spoke again, her voice sounded too loud. "Tell me about going to see Jeremy. And you still haven't explained why you asked about McCord."

She listened as Chance related how he'd barged into Jeremy's house as though determined to find the woman who'd played him for a chump. He hemmed and hawed for a few minutes as he obviously tried to figure out if he should be candid and she assured him the time for dissembling was way over.

"You're right," he said. He took her hand and rubbed her knuckles with his thumb. "He told me to drug you."

"Drug me? With what?"

"Just a second, I think I still have—" he began as he patted his coat pockets and then added, "Yeah. Here they are. These look familiar?

"My old prescription for barbiturates," she said, recognizing the label.

"The plan was I give you the pills and take Charlie."

"He wanted you to kill me," she said bluntly.

"Yes. If I were you I'd get rid of those."

"No kidding," she said as she shoved the bottle in her own pocket. "Well, Jeremy wanting me out of the way so

I won't talk is nothing new. Why in the world won't he just divorce me? Pride? It doesn't make sense."

"Maybe you're an heiress and don't know it."

She laughed. It wasn't something she'd done a lot of lately and it felt kind of good. "No, that's not it. But he is getting awfully reckless sending a man he just met to do his dirty work."

"That's what's been bothering me," Chance said. "And why I asked about McCord. I'm wondering if he sent McCord up here right after Charlie was taken. Maybe McCord reported back that he'd seen Charlie. I don't know, but that might have caused Block to leap at the chance of sending a hothead like he thinks I am to take care of you. Then McCord takes care of me and whisks Charlie back to Boise. The people at White Cliff can't complain to anyone because they're the kidnappers and Block sends Charlie overseas to boarding school."

"Is that his plan? Did he say that?"

"Yes."

"That jerk."

"For all we know, McCord already found Charlie and we're being set up. I murder you, McCord murders me. But if we live through all of this, I can testify what he wanted me to do to you. You can bring charges and get rid of him for good."

Like it was that easy, Lily thought to herself with little hope she and Charlie would ever be free of Jeremy's manipulations. "If McCord is here somewhere, he has to realize by now that you haven't killed me and maybe he reported that back to Jeremy."

"I suddenly feel like I have a target on my back," Chance said.

"Welcome to my life," Lily murmured.

"You should realize we're undoubtedly locked outside the gate by now," he added.

"I didn't think of that," Lily said as she noticed a brass lock attached to the trunk's hasp. "I wonder what someone is hiding in here," she mused aloud.

"I'll bring my gun next time and shoot off the lock," he said.

"And bring all that ground up above us down here? No thanks." She peered up the tunnel again, then at Chance. The thought of going back to that drab apartment to wait until morning was just too much to bear and that was if they could even get through the gate. "Maybe it's time to call it a night," she murmured.

"I'd like to know where this leads."

"I know, me, too. But how does that help Charlie?"

"I'm not sure, Lily. But how do we know it doesn't?"

She was quiet for a minute or two before adding, "We could come back sometime after Charlie is safe."

"That's true." They sat contemplating their own private thoughts until Chance stood up and pulled Lily to her feet. "If you want to go back, we'll go back."

She wasn't sure what to do. What was right and what was wrong? She looked into the dark and then up at Chance. "Let's give it a little longer," she said.

"Okay."

Twenty minutes later, the floor of the tunnel started an incline and Lily began to hope they were close to the end. When the light finally glinted off a solid surface ahead, she felt like yipping with joy.

The lever was the same as the one at the church end of the tunnel, a simple handle built into the wall beside a hook on which to hang the lantern.

"What if this opens directly into somebody's house?" she asked as she caught Chance's hand.

"That seems unlikely to me," he said. "This tunnel is at least three miles long, maybe more, which means a lot of earth was moved when it was constructed. I'd wager someone used mining tools to build it. But even if it does lead into a house, it's pretty late now and whoever owns it is probably asleep. We'll just get a feel for where we are and leave, okay?"

She nodded and held her breath as the door swung open just as the other had. The space that appeared was cluttered with boxes stacked atop each other. Chance immediately started investigating the boxes and Lily noticed a path existed from the double metal doors at one end to the entrance to the tunnel. The building sported a domed roof and the air felt cold and dank. She could see no windows. The door on this side also consisted of shelves and they held yet more boxes with lettering she couldn't make out as Chance had taken the lantern with him.

She looked back into the tunnel, dreading the return trip underground, and that was when the light from the distant lantern reflected off a metallic surface. She felt around until she found a cylinder of some kind hanging from a hook right inside the door. Pulling it into the light, she found herself looking at a red-and-white soup can that rattled when touched. It turned out to have a false lid that she pried off with her fingernails. She dumped a key tied to a ribbon connected to a small medallion into the palm of her hand. She put the lid back on the can and replaced it.

Chance spoke from over her shoulder. "What's that?"

"A key I found in that phony soup can right inside the

tunnel entrance," she said. "It's kind of small. Suppose it goes to that trunk?"

"It might."

She handed it to him. "You take it. What did you find in the boxes?"

"They all seem to contain the same thing: food, canned or freeze-dried. The shelves are stacked with boxes of MREs."

"Military food?" she asked.

"Yeah. Meals Ready to Eat. Last forever. I think I know where we are. Come with me."

"Let's close this door, first, just in case." They spent several minutes looking for the lever that opened and closed this door from the outside. Chance finally came across it when he tried to lift a heavy box from the shelf. The effort triggered the mechanism and the door closed soundlessly. They left the lantern right outside the tunnel and then carefully picked their way across the pitch-black room. Chance finally slid what sounded like a metal bar. The door opened and night air, moist and fresh, greeted their faces.

Lily could see very little as it was quite dark, but here and there a light glowed through a window in the distance. "Where are we?" she asked.

"White Cliff. I asked Maria about these bunkers earlier today. She said they'd been built way back at the beginning of things and were now used to store stuff." He took Lily's hands. "I'm going to see that you get to your place safely, then I'm coming back here. I'll take the tunnel to Greenville and tomorrow I'll drive the truck up here. By then you'll have had a chance to make sure Charlie isn't at the school. Together we can go see Maria."

"I told them you were staying in my apartment. Won't they think it's odd when you're not there?"

"That can't be helped. I can't leave my truck all night at the diner and risk it gets towed. You'll have to tell them you changed your mind about having me stay with you. Tell them I dropped you off at the gate and you walked home alone."

"Okay, that should work. Where will you sleep?"

"In the truck. Don't worry about me."

They closed the door behind them and Chance took her arm. "Hopefully no one will notice us," he added as they carefully picked their way along the muddy path toward Jefferson Park. They didn't risk so much as Lily's little flashlight.

"Whose house is that?" Lily asked as they passed pretty close to the big white house at the hub of the community's wheel.

"The head honcho, Robert Brighton and I guess his wife, Maria's sister. Maria lives there, too, in the back with her boys." They paused in the shadows near the fountain, avoiding the solar powered spotlight directed on the three figures. "I don't know where your apartment is," he said. There wasn't a soul around.

"It's a block or two from the park, right in the middle of the town where they can keep an eye on me."

Eventually they got to her apartment. He leaned down and kissed her and her heart pounded. She'd been attracted to him since the first time she laid eyes on him. She'd been new to the ranch and standing outside with Charlie when Chance rode his horse into the ranch yard. There'd been snow on the ground and the air was cold so that both man and beast exuded clouds of vapor. Charlie had trembled at the sight—he'd never seen a horse before. Chance had gotten off his ride, stared into Lily's eyes and smiled, then he'd swung Charlie into his arms. She'd been about to protest this stranger manhandling her boy, but Charlie had grinned ear to ear and when, after Charlie agreed, they rode off with Charlie sitting in the saddle in front of Chance, her quiet, cautious child had actually squealed with delight.

Chance had captured her attention at that moment and she'd had to struggle with herself to keep from jumping out of the Jeremy Block frying pan and into the Chance Hastings spa ever since. Neither place offered protection or safety. One was just a hell of a lot nicer place to spend your time.

Her head seemed to spin and for one blinding moment she glimpsed herself as an outsider might. A slightly built woman kissing a tall man, comforted by his strength and power, trusting his plans.

What was she doing? Indulging him in some pointless quest while her son was held prisoner, while her husband plotted to kill her and banish their boy to a nameless, faceless school? Charlie would wither and die off by himself like that. He had one person to champion for him and somehow she'd allowed herself to do it so poorly that now she was as good as bound and gagged.

So much of life had been terrifying for so long. She had to fight the weakness that coaxed her back for an encore performance of the old Lily. The meek her, the one who leaned on broader shoulders.

"This is our first date," he whispered against her cheek.

She took a step back. She felt shaky as though waking from a nightmare. But she hadn't woken up yet, the nightmare was in full swing. It wouldn't be over until

Charlie and she were racing off to anonymity and this time she would not goof it up.

"You look unconvinced," Chance said. "Well, think about it. We moseyed about, we went shopping, we ate dinner, we made out in a parked vehicle and then we had an exhilarating stroll through a tunnel. Now I'm kissing you good-night on your doorstep. In my book, that's a date."

She'd been dating while Charlie was in the hands of kidnappers? Is that how Chance saw this night? Is that how she saw it? "It's been an...odd...day," she said.

"But tomorrow we're going to find Charlie," he assured her.

That's what I told myself this morning and I'm no closer than I was! It's not Chance's fault—it's my own. She murmured good-night as she quickly slipped inside her apartment and closed the door.

She emptied her pockets onto the counter, wincing when she saw the barbiturate bottle. Damn Jeremy to hell.

A rap on the door drew her attention and she sighed. She did not want to see or talk to Chance without some time apart to think. She opened the door intending to tell him to go away, but it wasn't him standing on her doorstep.

"May I come in?" the man asked and proceeded over the threshold before she could utter a word.

Chapter Nine

After five minutes of preoccupied walking, Chance turned around and retraced his steps to Lily's door. He raised his hand to knock and then dropped it. Once again he left only this time he kept going.

Of all the women, he had to be stuck on her. What in the hell was wrong with him? Okay, okay, it wasn't really him, it was her. Prickly and sensitive and utterly infuriating. For two cents, he'd…

He'd nothing. But there'd been a change in her before she closed the door. It was like she'd pulled the shades, turned off the light, retreated inside herself, shutting him away.

Apart from her now, he reviewed his behavior in light of the fact that her son was missing. Had he come across as a shallow beast interested only in his own pursuits? Damn it, didn't she know or trust him more than that?

The answer was so obvious it hurt. The answer was no. She'd proven it over and over again and she'd tried to warn him that was how she felt. Well, he wouldn't walk out on her or Charlie, but he had to get his mind out of the bedroom and fix this situation so he could go home where he wasn't constantly being second-guessed.

He entered the bunker and picked his way back to

the tunnel entrance, feeling around in the dark until he found the right box and the door swung open. A second later, entrance once more concealed, he jogged toward the church, his movement causing light from the lantern to dart over the dirt and boards. He kept up that pace until he got to the wide spot where he remembered the key Lily had found. Sure enough, it opened the lock on the trunk.

He lifted the lid with the sense of discovery almost everyone feels when unlocking a potential secret, but it was anticlimactic without Lily there to share it. Was that what he could look forward to from now on? Was this why his father kept getting married? Was being alone so terrible?

Hell no.

He hadn't known what to expect he would find in the trunk but it wasn't a half-dozen colorful spiral-bound notebooks, the kind kids take to school. He opened one of them and found it crammed with small irregular handwriting that was really tricky to read. At first he thought it was written in code, but then he decided that it was just borderline illegible. Here and there he could make out a word. He thumbed through the book looking for some clue to the writer's identity, disappointed it hadn't been more revealing.

And then a name popped out from the writing: Darke Fallon.

At last!

Interested now, he looked through each of the books and discovered the name reoccurred in each of them several times, always buried in the text. He squeezed his eyes closed for a moment to ease the burning sensation and tried reading again. Eventually he deciphered a whole page and realized Darke Fallon was the hero in what appeared to be a poorly written and sexually explicit series of adventure stories. In the passage Chance read, the Fallon character risks certain death to kill a man threatening his beloved.

A beloved named *Tabitha*.

"Damn," Chance said to himself. That girl gets around! So did she come here or did someone from here go to the church? Judging from the bed on one end and the small trunk in the middle, someone from White Cliff went to Greenville. Unless someone from Greenville knew about this tunnel and used it as a hiding place for his or her work.

Okay, so Darke Fallon wasn't a real person, was that what this meant? He was a character created by someone with a good imagination and exceptionally poor writing skills? If that was true, it would explain why the police hadn't been able to track him down. Chance rubbed his eyes again. He was tired deep down inside and it was getting hard to think.

Maria had teenage boys, one of whom Betsy Connor said was cute. He'd met Dennis, a nice enough looking kid, but he seemed kind of unworldly when it came to relationships, and it was hard merging the image of a guy who spent his off time planning which new assault weapon he was going to buy with the lothario in the stories.

Had the person who created Darke Fallon been the same person who later killed Wallace Connor? Regardless of this fictional character, a real-life human had confessed and then killed himself and it was that man, no matter what name he gave, they had been unable to trace. Yet virtually on the eve of his competency trial, he'd chosen to die rather than come clean. Why? What, if anything, did these notebooks mean? Chance checked each again, looking for another name, but the only ones he could see were Darke Fallon and Tabitha. There wasn't a single thing Chance could see in any of the notebooks that identified who might have written them.

As he stacked the binders back in the trunk, he found a sealed envelope and an unopened packet of sunflower seeds. If the seeds were a clue, they seemed as generic as one could get.

But hadn't Dennis said something about his cousin liking sunflower seeds? Not step-cousin, either. Hadn't he mentioned smuggling bags of them out of his mother's store?

He opened the envelope and shook out a few photos with an old fashioned look to them. One was of an older woman with a long blond braid but the rest appeared to be trophies of hunts. A buck, a string of fish, quail.

He put everything back and relocked the trunk then continued on through the tunnel, debating whether or not he should call Lily and tell her what he'd found. If Fallon was a character written by someone who lived in White Cliff, then that could mean the family lived there just as they'd all assumed—and that would mean Charlie was close and maybe even safe. But if the notebooks belonged to someone from the Greenville end of the tunnel, everything got rearranged and without a name and an even larger population to deal with, where did that leave them?

It was beginning to appear they were going to have to bite the bullet and call the police and hope to God that Charlie wasn't caught in the middle. Lily had suggested that was just what she would do if this wasn't resolved soon and he didn't blame her.

Back at the church, he was relieved to find the maintenance room empty of randy teenagers. He moved quickly

but almost entirely in the dark as Lily had the tiny flashlight with her and he didn't dare take the lantern in case
someone missed it. The building looming above him
seemed very large and heavy with the past. It was ex-
tremely quiet as though it held its breath, so quiet he
could hear his feet crunch on something as he crossed the
maintenance room. His imagination supplied the image
of scattering cockroaches and he quickened his pace.

He received another surprise that night when he discovered the back door of the church was now locked
and couldn't be opened, even from the inside. He stood
there a second, trying to figure out if Tabitha or Todd
had locked it, and then decided it didn't matter. What
was important was to get out of there without becoming
entangled in some legal issue.

Another question sprang to mind as he searched for
a glimmer of light that would indicate a window facing
the back of the property instead of the street. The waitress at the diner had said Tabitha's grandfather used to
be a preacher. Had this been his church? If it had, was
he the one responsible for the tunnel? Who owned the
church now?

And what about those memorial grassy mounds built
by Thomas Brighton, Robert Brighton's father. The tunnel was old, the church was old, the mounds were old.
Was that where all the dirt that came out of the tunnel had
gone to: those mounds? If so, it would mean the White
Cliff end of things had originated the tunnel.

So what? That had to be decades ago, long before Lily
was born, to say nothing of her son.

His hand finally touched the cool smooth surface of
glass. He would have to break the window, he knew that,
and it worried him that if someone noticed, they would

find the glass outside instead of inside and know someone had been in here. He couldn't wait forever, though,
so with the quick decision-making prowess a man working with unpredictable animals his whole life learns to
hone, he wrapped his fist in his bandana and smashed it
through the glass.

The noise it made seemed way out of proportion to the
small hole he'd created. Using the bandana, he quickly
took out enough shards to get a hold of the boards nailed
to the outside. Eventually, he managed to loosen a couple of those and that resulted in additional broken glass.
It was a tight fit and a nine-foot fall to the ground once
he got through, but he got up quickly. There was no way
to replace the boards so they'd look exactly as they had,
but he propped them as well as he could and took the
time to sweep the broken glass on the ground beneath
the branches of the bush that had helped break his fall.

The good news was that the window not only did not
face the street, it didn't even face the back of the church.
Instead it was one of the windows on the wooded side
of the property. No one would notice it had been broken
unless they looked for it. He walked around to the street
and buried his hands in his pockets as he finally noticed
he'd cut himself in a few places. The walk back to the
diner and his truck was longer than he remembered and
he arrived there beginning to feel the effects of the miles
he'd put in that night.

Once in the truck, he took out his cell phone and saw
that it was three-fifteen in the morning. He wanted to
call Lily in the worst possible way, but she'd be asleep by
now and he wasn't sure she wanted to talk to him anyway. Instead he drove outside of Greenville where he'd
noticed a frontage road, found a spot under some trees

and leaned back in the uncomfortable seat. Twenty seconds later, he was out like a light.

HE AWOKE AT the crack of dawn with a stiff neck. It was very early, but he figured the bulk of White Cliff was already up and going. There was no better way to conserve power like electricity and gas than by adopting nature's light patterns as your own. Life was like that on the ranch quite often, as well, especially in the winter when frequent power outages were more likely.

He was anxious to see Lily and knew he couldn't wait until after she came back from the school. He wasn't sure if she intended on teaching her class today or just investigating. Last night it had sounded to him as though she'd lost all patience with playing this the White Cliff way, or his way, either, for that matter. As much as she feared he would muck things up by becoming a loose cannon, he feared she would do the same. Patience wasn't exactly the woman's middle name.

The guard let him in the gate and Chance drove directly to Lily's apartment. Her car wasn't parked where it had been the night before. Maybe school started early and maybe she'd driven to it. He wasn't sure exactly where the school was, but the community area wasn't that crowded—he should be able to find it. To be on the safe side, he knocked on her door in case there was another explanation about the car. He saw a note taped to the wood and read it. *Come see me*, it said. *I know about you.* It was signed *Maria*.

No one answered the door and as an afterthought, he twisted the knob in his hand and just about fell over when the door actually opened. The room was as impersonal as a generic motel room with the exception of a poster that showed the image of an automatic assault weapon being held aloft and the words *Get yours while it's still legal*. The bed was made and the dishes were done. There were no personal effects to be seen. Lily wasn't here and it didn't appear she was coming back.

"Don't jump to conclusions," he murmured. "Try the school." He hopped back in his truck. Happily, the town signposts were pretty clear about where things were. If he turned right, he'd apparently find an alternate route to Lake Freedom which he recalled seeing a sign for out on the road approaching White Cliff. Left would take him to Jefferson Park and the school was straight ahead. He wasn't foolish enough to think anyone would let him waltz into a classroom, but he could search the parking lot for Lily's car.

It wasn't there.

It hadn't been at Maria's store when he drove past. Was it possible Lily had somehow found Charlie last night and taken off without saying a word to him?

Hell yes, it was possible.

But it was also possible something else had happened to her. And if something had, the possible suspects included Jeremy Block, McCord, Charlie's kidnappers and maybe someone else he wasn't aware of. Where did he start looking?

A van drove up and stopped behind him. A fully armed man he'd never seen before hopped ably from the van and approached the truck on foot. Chance rolled down his window.

"Mr. Reed," the man said but it didn't sound like much of a greeting.

"Morning," Chance responded as amiably as he could. A movement in his mirror caught his eye and he saw two more men dressed in military fatigues and carrying weapons get out of the sliding door of the van. "Something I can do for you?" Chance added.

The man lifted his gun and pointed it at Chance's heart. "Come with us," he said.

Had he and Lily been seen coming and going from the bunker? "What's going on?" he asked.

"Robert Brighton has decided you are not White Cliff material."

"Okay, sure. If that's his decision, but I never met the guy so it seems unfair."

"It's the way it is," the man said.

"My wife is around somewhere," Chance added. "Just let me find her…"

"She has already left."

"Wait a second. Just—"

The other two men advanced. The one he'd been speaking to walked around and got into Chance's passenger seat.

"Drive to the main road, please," he said. His weapon was at ease, but Chance knew the guy would use it with little hesitation.

"Do you know what this is about?" Chance asked his passenger. He got no reply. They drove past the gate and then past Maria's little store. The store's neon open sign was dark. The other vehicle stayed glued to his bumper until they got to the misspelled sign about trespassing. Following barked directions, Chance stopped the truck and the man got out. "Keep driving and don't come back," the man said. Chance pulled onto the road. When he glanced in his rearview mirror, the gunman was still standing there, watching him.

He drove a mile or two and pulled off to the side. He tried Lily's cell phone, but she didn't respond.

As he figured it, these were the possibilities: she had taken off on her own and disappeared into the ether or she was still at White Cliff. If she was gone for good, she was gone. No way could he trace her again. In fact, he wouldn't chase her even if he knew where to go. The next time she left him, she left him for good.

But that was if she left willingly. He just couldn't believe she had, not without Charlie. And if she had Charlie, he could not believe she wouldn't have left him a message telling him so, especially after he'd accused her of being capable of such a thing.

If she was still at White Cliff, she needed help. Those folks had not been kidding around.

He got back on the road and took off for Greenville. Once in town he made a diversion to a department store where he bought fatigues and big clunky black boots. While he waited for change, he looked on the internet for a pastor Stevens, Greenville, Idaho, and found his first name was Roger. He searched for Stevens in Greenville and came up with one: Roger. The address given was a few blocks from the old church. He picked up a stepladder at the hardware store, ate the pastries out of the sack that he and Lily had bought the day before, then parked in front of a tidy redbrick house.

A knock was eventually answered by an old man in a severe black suit. A fringe of white hair surrounded his bald head and two very black eyes seemed to absorb everything in a single glance. It was almost impossible to believe this austere old guy was Tabitha's grandfather.

There was no time for pleasantries or subtle lead-ins to his questions, and Chance paused for a second, trying to figure out how to find out what he wanted. Too late he realized he should have just gone to city hall and looked it up.

"Yes?" the old guy said. He moved his hand and Chance saw that the book he held clutched to his chest was a frayed copy of the bible. "I don't have all day."

Chance offered his hand and introduced himself. His gesture was met with a stern frown and nothing else. "I came to ask you about your church," he finally said as he lowered his unshaken hand.

"I don't have a church anymore." Stevens started to close the door.

Chance hurried to say something that would stop him. "I mean your old church, Pastor. Or do you not keep that title after you stop preaching?"

"I keep the honorific, yes. And the answer to your question is that the good people of Greenville turned the building into a museum a few years back."

"The one a couple of blocks from here?"

"Not that one. That place was sold years and years ago. The buyer was very anxious to purchase it. Heard he paid a good penny and then just let it sit there and rot. The devil's handiwork, if you ask me."

"Do you know who bought it?"

"If I ever did, I've forgotten. Is that all? I have a full day of meditation planned."

"Your granddaughter," Chance began in order to confirm Tabitha still attended school, but the former pastor's demeanor immediately changed. His face turned red as he pointed a finger at Chance.

"You stay away from her, do you understand me?" he growled.

"Sir, no, no, you have this wrong—"

"I'm praying for her salvation. If I see you near her I will use my gun. Now get out of here." With that he almost slammed the door.

Chance stood there a second, the man's anger still vibrating in his head. Obviously he was aware of his granddaughter's exploits with the opposite sex, but did he really think Chance would be interested in a sixteen-year-old kid in that way? Man, he missed home at that moment. Gerard, Pike and Frankie would laugh their boots off if they'd witnessed this. He kind of shook himself free of the nasty feeling such an accusation can create in even an innocent man, and left. He wasn't going to take time to find the actual owners of the church. This had been another long shot that didn't pay off and he was antsy about Lily.

Carrying his new purchases, Chance parked around the corner from the old church, took his rifle out of the locked box in the back and hiked through the wooded property until he almost ran into the building. The stepladder gave him an easy climb to the broken window. Once inside, he hurried downstairs to the maintenance room. Pretty sure he'd come across the squished cockroaches he'd stepped on in the dark the night before, he found something else entirely. Sunflower seed shells. Not a lot, just a few…

Had they been there earlier in the evening when he'd come with Lily? They could have been. The little flashlight hadn't picked up many details, especially on the floor, and last night he'd been moving around in the dark. He wasn't sure what the shells told him. That the writer who stored his books in the tunnel had also come into this room? It was possible, of course, and if he had, maybe it had been to meet with the object of his desire: Tabitha Stevens. Chance had to talk to Tabitha.

He changed out of his jeans and boots and stuffed them into the empty bag from which he took the camouflage fatigues and boots. A few minutes later, he was dressed more or less like the men who had shown him out of White Cliff. He opened the closet and then the tunnel, stored all his stuff inside, closed everything up and slung the rifle over his shoulder.

It wasn't long before he wished he'd waited to change his shoes until he'd gotten to the far end. The tunnel was remarkably straight but he fervently hoped he'd never have to come this way again.

It took a little more nerve to open the door this time. If Lily had told Maria or anyone else about this passage, who knew who or what might be waiting for him? He turned off the lantern and hung it on the hook, activated the lever and opened the door into the twilight of the daytime bunker which was lit by a small skylight he hadn't noticed the night before. He made his way to the door and slid open the bar. Big sigh of relief. Now what? He straightened up, lowered the cap over his forehead to shade his eyes and started walking toward Jefferson Park, anxious not to be off on his own where he might draw attention.

Okay. Lily was not at her apartment, she was not at the school. Maria was not at work. Maria had left a note sometime in the past few hours saying she wanted Lily to meet with her but giving no details. Best bet? Lily was either visiting with or had been sequestered by Maria. And he knew where Maria lived.

He couldn't afford to wait until he figured out an escape plan. Technically, they had potential access to the tunnel, the unfinished wall and Lily's car. He would have to stay fluid and take whatever opportunity came along.

Nodding at but not making eye contact with a man dressed much as he was, Chance walked quickly to the big white house by the park. He took a sidewalk running parallel to the house and then one that took off at a right angle. In this way he was able to see the perimeter of the property. The house itself was easily as big as his father's place on the Hastings Ranch. The backyard was filled with large play-yard equipment, all of which appeared rusty and unused as though the children who had once played on them had outgrown the need to climb and swing. The exception was a single yellow toy tractor that someone had left near a sandbox. It looked brand-new, the paint bright, the color of the sun, the color of happy. It provided a jarring note in the forgotten play yard.

He found the addition on the back where he assumed Maria's family lived. Lily's car wasn't in evidence. He kept walking and found a detached garage. Next to that was a garden area where dozens of withered, dying sunflowers spilled their seeds onto the earth. He peered into the garage found a van and a truck and an equal weight of canned supplies piled on shelves. But he also discovered Lily's red coupe hidden under a tarp and his feeling of foreboding escalated.

Wishing he'd thought to bring the handgun, he spent a moment studying the house from the cover of the garage. The back door was directly in front of him, but you had to let yourself into the play area to access it. Most likely, the kitchen window was at the back of the house as well where a parent could keep an eye on playing children and garden alike. Early on a weekday morning, the chances of someone being in the kitchen seemed pretty high. Better to try the front.

He made his way as quickly as possible to the front of the house, once more passing that bright yellow tractor. He walked up the path, keeping his head down. Once on the porch, he sidled up to the plate-glass window and chanced a quick glance inside.

Lily sat on the sofa. There didn't seem to be anyone else in the room with her. She had her eyes closed and a shot of alarm blasted through him. He moved back to the door, tried the knob. The door opened soundlessly but some sixth sense or change in temperature must have alerted Lily she was no longer alone because her eyes flew open.

The first expression in her eyes was one of profound relief. The second was anxiety. "Chance? Get out of here!" she whispered. He finally saw that her hands and ankles were tied. "It's a trap!"

He crossed the room quickly, knelt to untie her feet.

"Go," she said.

"Not without you. Is Charlie here?"

"I was told that he was, but I haven't seen him."

"Why did they tie you up?" Her feet were free and he started on her hands.

"McCord is here," she said.

He pulled her to her feet. "Come on—"

"I can't leave," she protested. "Charlie might be here. I'm not going anywhere without him."

"Neither one of you is going anywhere," a man's voice said, and Chance turned to see McCord standing nearby. Chance had been so distracted he hadn't heard the man's approach. McCord held a gun pointed at Lily. "Lay your weapon on the floor and back up," he told Chance.

Chance looked back down at Lily, then settled the

rifle on the sofa and the two of them stepped away. A younger man showed up at the front door. "Everything okay, Dad?" he asked.

"Fine, Seth. Come inside and close the door. Take the gentleman's rifle with you. You might start a pot of coffee and wait until I call you, okay?"

"Sure." Seth closed the front door and walked past Chance and Lily. He grabbed the rifle off the sofa and left the room.

"What have you done with Robert Brighton?" Chance asked, but even as he posed the question, he thought he knew the answer. The McCord who stood ten feet away now did not appear much like the old boxer Chance had seen smoking a cigarette after Charlie's abduction. He must have worn lifts in his shoes at Block's house because he was at least two inches shorter than he'd been. His voice didn't sound as gravelly, either, and there was no trace of a limp as he moved. "You're Robert Brighton, aren't you?"

"Yes."

"What were you doing working for Jeremy Block?"

"I was undercover, just like you are now. You aren't really Pete Reed and this lady is not your wife, Dorrie Reed. She's Block's wife, Lily, or at least that's who you think she is."

Chance glanced at Lily. What did that last comment mean? She apparently wondered the same thing. "I have no idea what he's talking about," she said.

"Has he hurt you?"

"No."

He met Brighton's gaze head-on. "What's going on here? Where is Charlie?"

"All in good time. First tell me your real name."

"Chance Hastings. Why did you bring Lily here?"

"To lure you. I recognized your face from the night Charlie disappeared. I saw you out by the grape arbor. And then you show up here telling lies."

"You let me escape that night," Chance said.

"Yes. I assumed you'd come with Lily. I hoped you might even prove to be a good diversion, but Jeremy Block never guessed anyone helped Lily escape, just as he didn't guess that I drugged the nanny so she'd sleep through Seth and his brother climbing into Charlie's room and taking him."

"You took him!" Lily said.

"I arranged it, yes."

"Where is he?"

"First things first," Brighton mumbled. "You'll see him soon."

Lily's gaze was bouncing around the room as though her maternal instincts enabled her to see through walls to find her child. "He's been here all this time? Nearby?"

"Yes."

She glanced at Chance and his heart ached for her. "Maria left a note on your door," he said, hoping to ground her. "Apparently she came to see you sometime after you were brought here. Have you spoken with her?"

"No. This man was waiting for me last night when I returned to my apartment. He brought me here and locked me in a bedroom, then this morning he set this trap because he wanted to catch you off-guard."

"At about the same time he was setting this trap," Chance said, "someone sent a van full of armed men to escort me off White Cliff property. They said you had already left." He looked at Brighton and added, "Was that you?"

Alice Sharpe   157

"No. What has Maria got to do with any of this?"

"Quite a bit," someone said from yet another door that had opened off a hallway. A woman entered with the aid of a four-prong metal cane to prop herself up. McCord immediately went to help her. With his aid, she made it to an overstuffed recliner and sat down, her ankles and legs red and swollen where they peeked from beneath the hem of her robe. Chance and Lily might have been able to make it to the door to try to escape, but Chance knew he wasn't going anywhere until some basic questions received answers. This was as close to Charlie as they'd come, he was sure of it, he could feel it deep in his bones. And from the way Lily had tilted her chin, he was pretty sure she wasn't going anywhere, either.

The newcomer looked nothing like Maria, though she did look faintly familiar to Chance. Of course. It was her picture in the trunk in the tunnel. Younger in the photo by a couple of years, healthier for sure, but the same woman.

She obviously had some kind of circulation issues and breathing difficulties. Her long hair was faded blond and caught in a braid down her back. Her face was unlined, her skin almost translucent. Her breathing was labored. Two little hoses fed oxygen into her nose via a portable machine she carried in a sling near her body. She looked as if she'd been battling an illness or chronic condition for a long time and it was getting the best of her. It was hard not to feel for her and for the man who stood fussing over her.

"This is my wife, Elizabeth," McCord finally said as he straightened up after tucking a blanket around her lap. "Honey, you shouldn't have gotten up without someone to help. Perhaps you should go back to bed."

"I heard voices," she said. "I was hoping Maria had

come back. I told her about…everything…and she came unglued."

Brighton looked fondly at Elizabeth but there was also contrition in his eyes. "My dear, this young woman is Lily."

His comment was met with stunned silence and then finally a gasp. "*This* is Lily Block?"

"I prefer my maiden name," Lily said. "Kirk."

"You're different," Elizabeth said in awe, then looked up at McCord. "Robert, you said she was a heavy drinker, a druggie."

"She was strung up on something the night she came to Block's house."

Lily laughed with no humor. "I was strung up on nerves. I was scared and worried sick about my son."

He studied his hands for a moment then murmured, "Yes, I can see that now."

Elizabeth wasn't finished. "You said she couldn't be trusted. Then Maria found those pills so I told her what I knew…but this girl isn't like that. She's different than you said. Different from what Maria thinks!"

"Yes," Robert Brighton mumbled and shook his head. "I can see that. I don't know how—"

"Please," Lily said, looking from one person to the next. "Please, everyone, just stop talking. Where is my son? Do you know?"

"Why don't you sit down," McCord suggested.

Lily walked over to Elizabeth's chair and knelt down beside it. "Can you tell me where Charlie is? What does Maria have to do with any of this? Who is Darke Fallon?"

"So many questions," Elizabeth said.

"Then just answer one," Lily pleaded. The hope mingled with fear in her voice made Chance's heart clench. "Do you have my son?"

Elizabeth touched Lily's hair in an almost maternal gesture. "I did have him," she whispered, "but I don't anymore."

Chapter Ten

"We don't have him?" Robert Brighton said, and to Lily's ears he sounded surprised and upset by the news. "What the hell happened?"

Chance put his arm around Lily as he helped her stand. "Hang in there," he said. "We'll get to the bottom of this."

She looked up at him and took a breath, then she spun around and looked at the older woman. "What did you do with my boy?"

Elizabeth's lips trembled. "My sister took him."

"Maria? Where did she take him?"

"I don't know. She just said he couldn't stay here."

"But there's nowhere else for him to go," Lily protested. "The only person left is Jeremy." She gasped. "She wouldn't take him there, would she?" When Elizabeth didn't respond, Lily's voice climbed. "Would she?"

"No, no she hates him as much as I do. But maybe if she felt there wasn't an option."

Lily turned to Robert. "Give me my phone. I have to try to intercept her. I have to talk some reason into her."

"Maria doesn't have a cell phone," Elizabeth said. "Please, another few minutes isn't going to make any difference. Everything is so messed up. Let us explain."

Chance took Lily's hands in his. "We have to listen.

Maybe there's something that will help us get Charlie back. Please, Lily, trust me one more time and give these people fifteen minutes, then we'll figure out what to do next."

"Fifteen minutes," she said.

Chance sat down, pulling Lily to sit beside him. She was too upset for this inactivity. All she wanted to do was run out that door and keep running until she found Charlie.

But which direction did she run? Maria could have gone anywhere. And if she did do the unthinkable and returned Charlie to his father, then what? Jeremy would immediately secret Charlie away.

It didn't matter, she decided. She was ready to stand her ground and press charges and win her son once and for all. She had nothing to lose now, nothing.

"What Lily heard of the note you left after abducting Charlie seemed to indicate White Cliff and retribution for a lost son, an eye for an eye thing," Chance said.

"That's right," McCord agreed. "We aren't heartless. We figured if Jeremy knew we had Charlie that he wouldn't really worry about the child being harmed."

"How did you know he wouldn't call the FBI?" Lily asked.

"Because I know him," Elizabeth said. "I know what a coward he is. I knew he wouldn't risk public knowledge of his link to White Cliff and what he thinks is a nest of crazy people and I knew he wouldn't shed too many tears over his son. With him it's all pride."

"What about me?" Lily couldn't stop from saying. "I've been in hell. What about Charlie?"

"We had a mistaken opinion of you," Elizabeth said with a note of regret in her voice. Or maybe apology.

"We'd heard you abused drugs. Then you got here and told us a phony story but you acted pretty reasonable until your supposed husband came and then you and he just disappeared. Maria went to your apartment to see you this morning, but you didn't answer the bell. She taped a note to your door and then saw that the door was unlocked so she tried it. She found the barbiturates. She packed up your things, and came to me. After I told her about you, she was desperate to get you out of White Cliff. She didn't know Robert had already brought you here."

"I don't do drugs," Lily said. "Jeremy created that story to discredit me. He gave those drugs to Chance to kill me. And I was anxious because someone took my five-year-old child," she added. "*You* took him."

"After we got away from Block," Chance added, "we decided to look for a family who had lost a son. We kept coming up with the name Fallon. Lots of Fallons around, but none with a family member named Darke, not even one with a missing family member. It seemed this guy didn't exist. As far as I know, the police are still searching for his past. What we deduced brought us to you people. We didn't announce our true identities because Block had warned us that to do so would threaten Charlie's life. Was the man claiming to be Darke Fallon actually your son, Elizabeth?"

"I don't have a son," she said bitterly.

"But you did, didn't you? That's why the note you left when you took him said a son for a son. When Maria pointed out this house, she said Brighton lived here with her sister and his kids. But she originally phrased it 'their' kids. I think you had a son and I think he killed himself in a jail cell."

Chance turned to Lily. "There's something you don't know. I investigated the trunk in the tunnel."

"What tunnel?" Elizabeth asked.

"The one in the food storage bunker?" Robert Brighton asked.

"Yes."

"It leads to an old church my father bought three decades ago," Brighton explained. "He constructed the tunnel as another way out of White Cliff if authorities ever tried to take us over. I haven't thought about it in years."

"I'm betting your son knew about it," Chance said. "The trunk is full of stories with one central hero named Darke Fallon. There are also sunflower seeds."

"Darke Fallon," Lily whispered.

"Jimmy loved sunflower seeds," Elizabeth said with a choked sob. "I planted them this year just as I do every year." As Chance withdrew the key complete with its ribbon and small brass medallion from his pocket, she all but gasped. "Let me see that," she demanded. "That's my father's war medal. This is the key to his old trunk. We keep it in the basement."

"I doubt it's in the basement anymore," Chance said. "You said the trunk was full of stories?"

"Yes."

"Why would Jimmy hide his stories?"

"Perhaps because they were blatantly explicit."

"In what way?"

"Sexually. He apparently had a relationship or wanted one with a local girl named Tabitha Stevens."

"Tabitha?" Lily said, looking at Chance. "I saw initials in a heart by that cot in the church: J.B. plus T.S. It seems if that was Jimmy, he didn't tell Tabitha about the stories or his alter ego. Did Jimmy run across Tabitha in the church's maintenance room?"

"It seems likely," Chance said. "I found remnants of sunflower seeds on the floor. Plus, Tabitha's grandfather preached there at one time, perhaps she heard stories, I don't know." He looked at Elizabeth and added, "By the way, Tabitha was also Wallace Connor's girlfriend."

"Are you suggesting Jimmy killed Wallace Connor out of jealousy? We had proof Jimmy was here in White Cliff that day. That damn Block destroyed it."

"I'm not suggesting anything," Chance said. "But why didn't your son's fingerprints show up when the police checked files? Why no birth certificate, no social security card? Why did he lie about himself and why did this whole community never mention one of theirs died at the same time as the man everyone was asking them about? Didn't anyone put two and two together?"

"The first part is easy," Elizabeth said. "I had Jimmy after a very short and violent first marriage. I was so gullible. I left before I even knew I was pregnant and almost immediately met Robert. His father was in the midst of creating this alternate world. He'd been in prison because of a couple of scams he committed earlier in his life so he was keeping this place under wraps, knowing he'd be investigated when the police found out he was collecting money from investors.

"All that aside, White Cliff seemed like utopia to me. Robert already had several children by his first wife who died before we met. It seemed like I'd turned my life around and found my own little slice of heaven. Jimmy was born up here at White Cliff." She wiped at her eyes. "It seems like only yesterday. He was my only child.

And to answer your question, no, I didn't register Jimmy's birth."

"The government of this country is into every aspect of every life," Robert Brighton chimed in. "It doesn't matter what so-called party they belong to, they're all the same. They amass numbers and data and make records so they can control us. They conspire with foreign agents to undermine any expression of independence. Freedom is a concept to them and not one they particularly even like. We *live* freedom."

"That's why I didn't get him a social security number or anything else. As far as the world outside of White Cliff knew, he didn't exist and it seemed like the most pure form of freedom I could gift him with. As time passed, it became clear that we'd made a good choice because Jimmy was different than other kids. He loved to hunt and fish but he was poor in school and awkward around people. Other kids made fun of him at times. I can't tell you how many fights we broke up. I knew he was roaming around at night but I also knew he couldn't get through the gate and the unfinished part of the fence is guarded… I didn't know he wrote stories and I would have sworn girls were the last thing in the world he would concern himself with."

"Boys will be boys," Robert said. "I should have known that. I just had no idea he'd found the tunnel. But how do you know for sure it was Jimmy who wrote those stories?"

"It stretches the imagination to think someone else created those stories and the character Darke Fallon and then got your son to confess to murders using that same name," Chance said. "Plus, there's a photograph of you in the trunk, Elizabeth. We need to verify everything, though.

Perhaps you'll recognize his handwriting. It's very hard to read."

"Like a scribble?" Elizabeth asked.

"Yes. But I still don't get it," Chance added. "Someone here must have seen Jimmy's picture in the newspaper when police were attempting to track Darke Fallon down."

"It was a terrible picture," Elizabeth said. "Most of the people here probably didn't even see it. Most of us believe the government runs the media. Some did, but didn't recognize Jimmy, they just assumed the police had a man in custody named Darke Fallon, and no one had ever heard of that person before. A few people did recognize Jimmy's photo and asked us about it. We told them it was a conspiracy by the police to undermine White Cliff's legitimacy, an attempt to gain access to our community assets and records. We said Jimmy was a victim just as much as the Connor boy and nothing would be gained by admitting he came from here. Anyway, what business was it to the police that our boy had sacrificed himself for some reason we'll never know?"

"Dead is dead," Robert Brighton said. "If the police invade White Cliff, there will be more violence. I have to believe that Jimmy would not want his brothers and sisters dying because of a decision he made."

Lily stared at the Brightons and realized they were on a different planet than she was, not only politically, but in other ways, as well. Charlie's welfare was all that mattered and if anything happened to him, she'd move heaven and earth to avenge him. "What was your evidence that Jimmy wasn't in Boise?" she asked.

"A dated photograph."

"Don't you have the negative or a copy of it on your computer?"

"No, it was one of those old Polaroids," Elizabeth said. "Jimmy found a camera and a whole box of film down in the basement, left there by Robert's father decades ago. He liked to fool around with it. Anyway, Jimmy was ice fishing that day over at Freedom Lake with his stepbrother."

"Then you have a witness," Chance said.

"Yes, but it's doubtful a relative, even a step relative and especially someone from White Cliff, would be believed in America's skewed justice system. What we had was that photograph."

"Of him fishing?"

"Of him with his catch, yes. We ate his fish for dinner that night. He seemed right as rain. The next morning he was gone like he'd been teleported off the face of the earth. A day after that, he confessed to a murder that happened while he was up at Freedom Lake. Maria drove down there with the picture a day later. Jeremy assured her he would use it to help solve the case. She also told him something he didn't know that we hoped might motivate him to work harder on Jimmy's behalf. By the weekend, Jimmy was dead."

"He must have left during the night via that blasted tunnel," Brighton said. "I should have thought of that. It's just been years since anyone talked about it."

"All of this is interesting," Lily said. "But it's been over fifteen minutes. I'm sorry about your son, but it's my son we have to think of now."

Robert had been sitting on the edge of a chair and he got to his feet as though he couldn't sit anymore. "You have to understand…Elizabeth hasn't been the same since Jimmy died. And now she's sick… I thought if I could bring her Jeremy's boy it would give her a reason to keep fighting."

"But why Charlie in particular?"

Robert looked at Elizabeth. "She has to know, honey."

"Know what?" Lily said.

"I never divorced my first husband, Lily, so I'm not really Robert's wife," Elizabeth said. "There's no easy way to tell you this." She took a deep breath and kept going. "I married Jeremy Block right out of high school and left him less than a month later. That's what Maria told Jeremy the day she gave him the photo, hoping it would make a difference to him. But…it didn't."

"Wait a second," Lily said. "Your son Jimmy is my Charlie's half brother?"

"Yes."

"After Jimmy's death, I got a job working for Jeremy," Robert said. "We knew he had a son—we didn't know his mother had taken him when she left. And then, lo and behold, the son is returned, rescued from his hard-drinking, drug-taking, carousing mother down in Reno…"

"None of that is true except that I lived in Reno," Lily said.

"We know that now," Elizabeth murmured. "I should never have trusted a word that man said. But that's why Robert and the boys took Charlie as soon as Jeremy got him back. To protect him from his parents."

"I thought it only fair that Jimmy's half brother have a better life," Robert said.

Chance sprang to his feet. "Jeremy Block is a bigamist?"

Elizabeth nodded.

"That's why he wouldn't divorce me—we weren't actually married," Lily said. "He couldn't go to court and have that come out. Didn't he know all he had to do was tell me that? I would have danced in the streets."

"He didn't want you to dance in the streets," Chance said.

"But what good does this do us?" Elizabeth said.

"Don't you see?" Lily demanded, staring right into her eyes. "Jeremy can no longer deny his past and his current behavior. With two of us to tell the world—"

She stopped talking because Elizabeth was shaking her head. "The only reason I'm alive is that Jeremy can't get to me in here. We allowed you entrance to White Cliff because Robert had met you at Jeremy's house and we were curious to see what you wanted, especially when you lied about yourself. We let Mr. Hastings in because Robert recognized his face on our surveillance camera from that night we took Charlie. No one else gets in here."

"Elizabeth," Lily pleaded, "listen to me. When you decided that your son's death was something to be privately mourned and laid to rest, you were robbing society of finding the true murderer of a young man. That murderer is still out there after having gotten away with a heinous crime. Maybe they'll strike again and someone else will die. And for your son to have taken the blame—it had to be someone he trusted and cared for deeply."

"Someone like Tabitha Stevens," Chance said, meeting Lily's gaze.

"Yes. Or her boyfriend Todd or even Betsy. How do we know who Jimmy met and what he got himself into?" She turned back to Elizabeth. "You've let hiding become a way of life for you. I understand, I did the same thing. But it's time to make Jeremy pay for his past, time to protect innocent people from his manipulations, time to stand up." All this sounded righteous enough but it rang hollow. Charlie was halfway back to Boise by now.

"Why did you let Maria take the boy?" Robert asked Elizabeth.

"I didn't *let* her," Elizabeth said, looking up at him. "She panicked when she found the drugs in Lily's room and then when she heard you had abducted her and brought her to this house, she went nuts. She grabbed the boy and said she had to find somewhere else to take him, that he would ruin everything for everyone if he stayed here. I heard him beg to see his mommy. Why didn't I listen to him?"

Lily knew why. Elizabeth hadn't listened to Charlie or her own common sense because she hated Jeremy with an unabated passion. Her desire to hurt him overrode her ethics and morals and who got to pay for it? Charlie, that's who.

Lily had steeled herself not to break down, but it was a struggle to hold back the anger. How could Maria have done this? But there was another unavoidable consideration. What would have happened if Lily had been honest with everyone from the get-go? It had seemed like such a horrible risk, one she'd been unable to take, and now look where it had all ended up.

They stood or sat in an informal circle, staring at their hands or their feet, no one willing to meet anyone else's gaze. Lily took Chance's hand. It was time for them to return to Boise and the authorities, time for Lily to face the warrant and then press charges, time to fight for her child before he disappeared out of the country.

He looked down at her and seemed to understand what

she was thinking. He put his face next to hers but just then the door banged open and they all turned in shock.

Maria stood on the threshold. For once, she did not look calm and controlled. Her eyes grew huge as she looked at Lily, and Lily's heart sank.

"Where is he?" Lily demanded, stepping toward Maria. "Where is Charlie?"

Maria finally tore her gaze from Lily and looked at her sister. "I didn't know where to take him," she said. "He started sobbing when I mentioned his daddy. I couldn't take him there."

"Thank goodness," Elizabeth said. "We've been all wrong about Lily."

"I found a whole bottle of pills in her room just this morning," Maria said, suspicion and judgment harsh in her voice.

"I know you did, but there's a reason for that and it's not what you think. Where is the boy? He needs to be with his mother."

Maria looked from Elizabeth to Robert. "Just like that? You two put this whole community in jeopardy and now you're just going to let her take him?"

"Yes," Robert Brighton said. "That's what we're going to do."

Maria glanced over her shoulder at her car. That was enough for Lily who ran past her. Charlie was curled up on the backseat. She opened the door and sat beside him, just taking a second to catch her breath so she wouldn't add to his fear. Dark circles ringed his eyes, dried tears clung to his lashes. She ran her hand along his arm. He opened his eyes with a start and began to withdraw and then he saw who it was. Relief swept away the trepidation.

Holding him and rocking him, Lily kissed his cheeks

and peered into his eyes. His precious freckled face looked wan and tired but otherwise okay. Knowing she had been locked in a bedroom last night while Charlie had slept in another one in the same house stung deep, but in this instant of reunion, the pain subsided and Lily's heart seemed to burst in her chest. She buried her head against his warm little neck and uttered soothing words. "You're okay now, baby, you're safe, Mommy is here."

She was suddenly aware that Chance's hands were on her shoulders and he was leaning down. "Hey there, buddy," Chance said and Charlie tore himself from his mother's embrace and threw himself at Chance. As Lily got out of the car, she watched Chance lift her son in the air above his head. Charlie laughed and squealed and she was reminded of the first time Charlie met Chance. But now she also recalled the other sensation she'd had that day. This was how a relationship between a man and a small child was supposed to be: fun, exciting, liberating, not fraught with worry and tension. With Jeremy, Charlie had always known he wasn't quite good enough, he didn't measure up. Even if he couldn't articulate the concept, he felt it at the core of his being.

If she ended up in jail until things got straightened out, would the courts allow Charlie to stay with Chance and the others at the Hastings Ranch? With Gerard's Kinsey in residence and Chance's stepmother, Grace, around, there would be two women to nurture him and five men to teach him how to be a man.

Or would the courts hand him over to Jeremy? She had decided that if she ever got Charlie back, she would act responsibly and legally and strike to win in the courts no matter what the odds. But now that she had him, the temptation to run was so tantalizing it was scary.

Chance finally handed Charlie back to her. As she took him into her arms, Chance leaned down and kissed her briefly, then winked. "You're not married," he said.

"I know," she said as Charlie wiggled down to stand beside her.

"How fantastic is that?"

"Pretty darn fantastic." It didn't really solve any of the more pressing issues, but it felt great to know she wouldn't have to go through a divorce. In fact, between what Chance could tell authorities about Jeremy trying to pay him to kill Lily and what she knew about Jeremy's past now, especially in regards to bigamy and destroying evidence, it began to look hopeful there might be a light at the end of the tunnel. She would stay and fight.

They started to walk back to the house but Charlie grabbed his mother's hand and tried to hold her back. "I want to go home," he said.

"Did those people hurt you, honey?"

"No," he admitted with a trembling lower lip. "Seth is my friend. I just want to go home. I want to see Grandpa Harry."

Chance smiled. Harry Hastings was Chance's dad. He and Charlie had bonded during the summer.

"I know you do," Lily said wishing he hadn't named the Hastings ranch as his home. But what other options had she given him? A big, cold mansion with an uncaring father or the sublet in Reno? Neither held a candle to the Hastings ranch and she knew it. "We're not staying here," she assured him. "We just have to clear up a couple of things."

Chance leaned down and picked the boy up. "I'll hold on to you," he said. "No one is going to take you without your permission ever again, okay?"

"Promise?"

"Promise."

He wrapped his arms around Chance's neck and Chance smiled at Lily. He took her hand and they walked back inside the house.

Robert Brighton now sat on the sofa, Maria beside him, deep in conversation. Elizabeth looked up as the three of them entered and smiled. "You make a lovely family," she said.

"We're not actually a family," Chance said quickly.

Lily figuratively shook her head. Elizabeth's words must be terrifying to a confirmed bachelor like him. Between Charlie's innocent comment a moment before and now this bombshell, the poor guy was probably trying to figure out an exit plan. And hadn't she entertained a momentary fantasy outside when Chance lifted Charlie above his head?

"I've been thinking about what you said," Elizabeth added. "You're right. I need to clear Jimmy's name. I need to help find the true murderer. We need to see those journals and make sure they're Jimmy's."

Lily nodded. "I've been thinking, too. I took a bunch of stuff from Jeremy when I left him. It's locked in the trunk of my car. I know more now than I did when I went through it all before. Maybe if I look again, something will jump out at me."

"It's worth a shot," Elizabeth said.

Maria stood up and approached Lily. "I owe you an apology. With Robert gone for weeks at a time and Elizabeth struggling with grief and illness…it was terrible after Jimmy died. He and Dennis were pretty close. We were all shaken up and then not to even have his body to bury, to have to pretend…well, I almost left White Cliff.

I thought if that's the level of commitment required to live here, was it worth it?"

"A girl at the bakery mentioned that you withdrew after Christmas. That was after Jimmy died, wasn't it?"

"You're referring to Betsy. Nice girl. I didn't know she noticed. I just looked at my own sons and wondered... well, here we are nine months later and I was willing to do almost anything to protect this...this place. I'm getting paranoid."

That ought to make her fit right in at White Cliff, Lily thought. The whole place was paranoid.

"Now, I'd like to help," Maria declared.

"Then get the envelopes of data and things out of my car," Lily said, "and help Elizabeth and I look for something I can show the police. I'll do everything I can to downplay your community's involvement. Jeremy has to be discredited for all our sakes."

Chance looked at Brighton. "Why don't you and I go get that trunk and bring it back here? And then I need to find Tabitha Stevens and see what she knows about Jimmy. It's suddenly occurred to me that the moment this goes public, she might be in danger from Wallace Connor's murderer."

Chapter Eleven

Two hours later and Elizabeth, tears still streaming down her face from finding her photo in with her son's things, confirmed the notebooks were filled with Jimmy's handwriting. They'd each thumbed through the almost illegible raucous events of Jimmy's rich fantasy life looking for clues as to the identities of any other people Jimmy might have met. Even Seth had offered to help and though he had to be in his early twenties, he blushed more than once as he waded through his dead stepbrother's words.

When Maria's son, Dennis, showed up, greeted Chance and offered to help read, his mother sent him to the kitchen to make sandwiches. "He's too young to read this stuff," Maria said, glancing at the open notebook on Elizabeth's lap. "Heck, I think I'm too young."

"You could knock me over with a feather," Elizabeth said as Maria left to help Dennis. "I had no idea my boy had such an imagination."

Chance looked at Lily and a kind of communication raced between them. The events were way too graphic for a kid without experience to be able to make it all up. It sure seemed to Chance as though Tabitha and Jimmy had had a torrid affair. How many other people knew about it? Was Wallace Connor killed because he found out and tried to put a stop to it? But why down in Boise? And if it was true Jimmy couldn't have murdered him, then who?

"I don't understand what Jimmy was doing in the Connor van all the way down in Boise," he said aloud.

"No one does," Brighton said.

Chance checked his watch. He'd tried calling Tabitha's grandfather an hour ago to urge him to pick her up from school and keep her under his watchful gaze, but the phone had gone unanswered and truthfully, Chance had almost been glad. He wasn't looking forward to the old guy's supposition that Chance was lusting after his granddaughter.

After the sandwiches, Charlie fell asleep on the sofa between Lily and Seth with his tractor clutched in his small hands. Lily sorted the papers she must have looked at a dozen times already. "Any luck?" Chance asked her.

"No." She picked up a stack of photos and flipped through them. "Pretty girls, fast-looking boats, dead fish...wait a second. Elizabeth, describe the photo you sent with Maria. Better yet, I'll describe it to you. A young man's profile, three pretty large fish displayed on a newspaper, a hole in the ice and the left half of a sign that says Freed La. I take it that's the sign on Freedom Lake?"

"You have the photo?" Elizabeth cried. "Let me see it."

Chance took it from Lily so she wouldn't have to disrupt the sleeping child and handed it to Elizabeth. There wasn't a doubt in his mind that it was a Polaroid.

"This is it! Robert, this is it! If you get a magnifying glass, you can see that the paper is dated the same day the Connor boy was killed in Boise."

It was on the tip of Chance's tongue to point out the police might claim the photo could have been staged and taken at a later date using an old newspaper and then he realized that was impossible. Jimmy had turned himself in the day after this newspaper was printed and had not come back to White Cliff ever again. It wasn't the kind of photo that could be doctored, either. The technology in the old Polaroid instant camera was ancient by today's standards.

Brighton looked concerned. "The police will show up in White Cliff," he said. "My father would roll over in his grave if he knew."

"Then I suggest you preempt some of the trouble by going to see them yourselves," Chance said. "Be open and up-front, don't hide the truth. This will eventually be figured out. Jimmy will be exonerated and the true culprit will be caught."

"You really believe that, don't you?" Brighton said.

"Yes."

"I was not raised to trust our government or any of its agencies."

"I was," Chance said, smiling to himself when he thought of his father's very firm opinions on the matter of authority. He was also thinking to himself that a lot of people he knew personally were uptight about the police getting into the middle of their lives until someone robbed, cheated or bashed them over the head, something no one here would think of doing. The White Cliff people seemed to live what they preached.

He took out his cell phone and snapped a picture of the photograph. Now he would have something to show the police in Greenville, something tangible to show Tabitha and hopefully elicit her grandfather's understanding.

"I've got to drive into town," he said as he stood.

Charlie woke up just then and upon hearing Chance's

words, rubbed the sleep from his eyes with his fists. "Don't go, Uncle Chance," he said.

Lily hushed him. "How about we come along with you?" she asked, looking up at Chance.

"Sure," he said, glad for the company. He didn't look forward to talking to Pastor Stevens again.

"Will you come back here after you've done what you need to do?" Brighton asked.

"Yes."

"Considering everything we've put you through, I consider that a leap of faith."

"So do I," Chance said. "Don't forget it."

IN THE END, Seth rode along with them in Lily's car, Chance at the wheel. He was very pleased to have Lily beside him though there was an undercurrent between them now. Charlie had been the pivotal force before, his safety and welfare triumphing over any other concern. But now that he was safe, there was a whole lot to figure out.

They'd brought along a book or two so Seth offered to stay in the car and read to Charlie while Chance and Lily went to speak to the old pastor.

This time the tidy house had an abandoned feel to it as they approached. The front door stood ajar. Considering the heavy skies and dropping temperature it seemed an odd thing. Chance knocked on it while holding the knob. "I should warn you the good pastor believes I'm a pervert," he told Lily, who looked up at him with wide eyes.

"How did he figure that out about you so fast?"

"Ha, ha, very funny." He knocked again and then rang the bell.

"Maybe he's hard of hearing," Lily said.

"I don't think so. Anyway, it's late enough that his granddaughter is probably out of school." He stepped inside the house. "Pastor Stevens? Are you here? Tabitha?"

They heard the mewing of a cat coming from behind a closed door. Chance crossed the small, austere room, rapped on a connecting door with his knuckles, then opened it. A small gray cat darted between his feet and headed for the still open front door.

Chance barely noticed this because his gaze had returned to the room and what he saw there riveted him in place. Before he could warn her not to, Lily reached his side and looked past him into the room.

"Oh, no," she said with a gasp as her hands flew up to cover her mouth.

The pastor had been shot right through his heart while he sat at his desk with a half a dozen books lying open in front of him. The expression on his face telegraphed surprise, not horror. There was a lot of blood on the chair and the wall behind him. His open death stare told Chance that checking for a pulse was unnecessary, but he did it anyway and shook his head when he faced Lily.

"Where's Tabitha?" she asked.

"Good question. Look upstairs, I'll search down here. Try not to touch anything you don't have to touch."

"What about the police?"

"I'll call them."

He dialed 911 as he searched for Tabitha. There wasn't a single sign of her except for a backpack sitting by the door in the kitchen as though dropped there minutes before. Tabitha's initials were written on the shoulder strap. Lily showed up with an ashen face. "Someone who apparently knew the combination opened a gun safe in the pastor's bedroom. It looks like a handgun is missing. Did you get the police yet?"

"I'm trying. The signal is really weak. How about your phone?"

"I forgot to get it back from Robert Brighton."

"Wait, it's ringing," he said. As soon as he heard a voice, he reported the address and that there had been a shooting but he had no chance to deliver any details because the signal suddenly died.

"Let's use the pastor's phone," Lily suggested.

"I haven't seen one. Maybe he had a cell but I'm not checking his body to find it. Let's wait outside," he told Lily and took her hand.

They found Seth and Charlie standing on the sidewalk. Lily looked up at Chance and paused midstep. "I really don't want Charlie to see a dead body removed from this house. Frankly, I would rather he not even see the police. He's been through enough and this has nothing to do with him."

"Or Seth. Let's send them both back to White Cliff in your car. We can take my truck when we're finished here. It's parked over by the church."

"I can't believe I'm sending Charlie away with one of the people who kidnapped him," she murmured.

"Life is strange," Chance agreed. "You can leave yourself if you want to. I'll explain it to the cops."

"No. If I'm going to be the mother Charlie deserves, it better start here. I don't want anyone saying I ran out when my fingerprints are undoubtedly inside that house."

They explained things to Seth who was delighted to leave before the police arrived. Lily handed over her keys while Chance handed him a five and told him to buy ice cream on their way out of town. There were no arguments from Charlie as they drove away; Lily was the one near tears. Chance looped an arm around her shoulders and hugged her. "He'll be okay."

"I know he will. But I just got him back." She sighed deeply. "Chance, who killed the pastor, do you have any idea?"

"Suspicions," he said, "but nothing concrete enough to mention. What I really don't get is why." They stood there another ten minutes without hearing a siren. In that time, the clouds overhead grew increasingly ominous as though Pastor Stevens's wrath gathered in the heavens. "I'm wondering if my message got through to the police after all," Chance said at last.

"Should we go look harder for the pastor's phone?"

"Do you want to go back in that house?"

"No."

"Me neither. Wait here." He jogged up the path to the house and closed the door, then walked back to Lily. "The church is only two blocks that way," he said pointing. "Let's go get the truck and drive to the police station."

"Anything is better than standing here," she said and they fell into step. The clouds broke a few minutes into their walk, and they picked up their pace but there was no way to escape the downpour. Lily had her hooded coat, but Chance had stopped wearing his Stetson a couple of days before in an effort to blend in. The little fatigue cap wasn't enough to offer any protection, but he didn't really need any. How many cattle drives had included unexpected weather? Almost every single one. You just kept going.

He was digging in his pocket for his truck keys when Lily grabbed his arm and pulled him behind the same tree they'd hidden behind the night before.

"What's wrong?" he asked.

"I just saw Betsy Connor walk around to the back of the church."

"Uh-oh. That can't be good. I wish we knew for sure where Tabitha was."

"My money is on the maintenance room."

"Maybe. Okay, I'm going to get to my truck and take the gun out of the back. We've got to make sure Betsy isn't in trouble. Do you want to wait in the truck?"

She flashed him a wry smile. "What do you think?"

"I think you want to come with me but I also think you'd better consider what's good for Charlie. He needs his mom."

"Point taken," she conceded. They ran to the truck and Lily slid inside.

Chance took his revolver out of the locked case and handed her the truck keys. "If anything goes wrong, get yourself out of here, okay, Lily?"

"Chance, I—"

"Not now, sweetheart," he said. "I'm in a hurry. Lock the doors. I'll be back." He leaned inside and kissed her. Her lips were cool and wet and perfectly delicious. He tore himself away and ran toward the back of the church.

The back door stood open this time. He entered as quietly as possible, almost tiptoeing in the big black combat boots so his footsteps wouldn't be heard downstairs. Wet marks on the floor possibly belonged to Betsy. If so, she apparently hadn't known where to look first. The marks seemed to wander room to room as though she searched much the way he and Lily had the night before. Had it really been less than twenty-four hours ago?

The floor joists were solid and he heard no giveaway creaks or groans as he moved directly to the head of the stairs where he paused to listen for voices. What came next was a bloodcurdling scream and then a shot. All bets off now, he thundered down the stairs, cursing his earlier caution.

The maintenance room door stood open. Sounds of sobbing came from inside. He paused at the threshold, gun drawn, took a hasty glance inside and felt a chill race through his bones.

The glimpse into the room was a glimpse into hell. Betsy lay on the floor, unconscious and bleeding. Todd, who Chance had only seen once when he came into the bakery to visit Betsy, lay on the bed, half-dressed, bound and gagged and obviously dead. Tabitha stood by the furnace, a gun in her hand, her eyes dark and foreboding as she stared at Betsy's still form. She seemed oblivious to Chance's presence, her gaze only leaving Betsy when she darted a glance at what was left of Todd.

With his heart in his throat, Chance knelt down to check on Betsy and found the bullet had lodged in her shoulder. She opened her eyes as he touched her. It was obvious she recognized him. "Help me," she whispered.

"Stay still," he murmured and stood again. This time, Tabitha's gaze met his and he flinched. The girl's eyes were wild, her bloodred hair an obscene punctuation in this unholy mess. Mascara bled down her cheeks in black streaks.

"Give me the gun, Tabitha," he said gently.

"Why should I?" she demanded.

"You don't want to hurt anyone else."

She looked at the dead boy on the cot. "You mean him? He was two-timing me with that cow," she said, nodding toward Betsy. "He thought he was going to get some bondage sex. I fooled him, didn't I?"

"Yeah, you did. What about your grandfather?" Chance said, and took a small step forward, his goal to put himself between Tabitha and Betsy. Trouble was, the room wasn't that big and even worse, he was pretty sure he heard footsteps on the stairs. If Lily had responded to the sound of gunfire…if she came into this room…he couldn't let that happen.

"Stop right there," she said.

He did as she asked and raised his voice when he spoke to cover any noise Lily might make. "Your grandfather is dead. You killed him just like you did Todd."

"My grandfather was going to send me away. He knew about…things. He said I was a demon and had to be locked up. Me? Do I look like a demon to you?"

As a matter of fact, she did. Chance shook his head. "You look like a young woman in very deep trouble. Let me help you. Give me the gun."

"No," she said, crying now. "It's too late. It's been too late for a long time."

"I know about Jimmy Brighton," Chance said. "I know he didn't kill Wallace. I think you know who did."

"Jimmy," she said and for a second, there was a note of longing in her voice. "Why did he give the police that stupid, phony name?"

Probably to protect his family and White Cliff, Chance thought. But it was possible there was another reason as well. "Maybe it's how he thought of himself in relation to you—larger than life. He would have done anything for you."

"I know."

"How did you meet him?"

"One night after Wally left, the closet door suddenly opened and Jimmy was just here. I'd never seen him before. He said he'd hidden away and listened to us have sex many times and fantasized what I must be like but I was even more beautiful than he imagined. He was so strange but he was fascinated with me. He admitted he was a virgin but wow, you could have fooled me."

"Is that why you asked him to cover for you after you killed Wally?"

She shook her head violently as tears trickled down her cheeks.

"Tell me about it, Tabitha. What were you and Wally doing down in Boise?"

"I wasn't in Boise," she protested.

"I think you were. I think you went there with Wally. Why?"

It took her a few seconds until she resumed speaking through trembling lips. "I...got...pregnant," she mumbled.

"Was it Wally's baby?"

For a minute, it didn't look as though she would respond and then finally, she gave an almost imperceptible nod. "He said he would marry me. That's what I wanted. I wanted out of this town. Wally was older, he could stand up to my grandfather. It was perfect. Wally said we would run away to Mexico. But when we got to Boise, he bought a lot of beer and stopped at a motel. He snuck me into his room. He said it was to protect me because I was underage... We had some beer. He got stinking drunk and finally admitted he was really taking me down to Nevada because he knew someone there who would give me an abortion, no questions asked. I said no way. How could he lie to me like that? And then he told me to grow up and stop whining. He was going to dump me, I could see it written all over his face."

"You got in a fight," Chance said.

"Yeah. Eventually he passed out. I saw his knife and I picked it up and stared at it and then I stared at him… I don't know, he snorted in his sleep and something just… snapped. I went nuts. The next thing I knew, he was dead. I took his ring so it would look like he was robbed. I wasn't thinking real straight. I got in his van and drove home. There was a lot of blood on the steering wheel and the upholstery. It smelled like death in there. I smelled like death. I came here to see Jimmy. I told him… I told him the baby was his. He insisted on driving the van back to Boise and confessing…it just all got out of control. And then he killed himself!"

"And you lost your baby."

"Grandpa knew that's why I was sick. I told everyone it was because of Wally, but he just somehow knew I was lying. The truth was I hated Wally by then, I was glad he was dead, I would have killed him all over again if I had the chance."

Goaded by the rage that must have overcome her as she heard this description of her brother's death, Betsy suddenly pushed her way past Chance and screamed at Tabitha. Lily appeared in the doorway. Tabitha aimed the gun at Betsy, then apparently saw Lily as a larger threat and aimed at her. Chance didn't think twice. He fired his weapon. Tabitha screeched and dropped her gun as Betsy suddenly ground to a stop, one arm supporting the other, head bent forward, back heaving as her heavy sobs bounced off the walls.

Chance kicked Tabitha's weapon across the floor. He'd aimed for and hit her gun hand but she seemed impervious to everything, even pain, and stared right through him. He yanked what appeared to be Todd's shirt off the bed and wrapped it around her hand to stem blood loss. Then he put an arm around Betsy and led her to the door where Lily stood, eyes wide, gaze riveted to Todd's body on the cot.

"Lily," he said softly. "Lily?"

She tore her gaze from the cot and looked up at him. "It's so terrible," she whispered. "It's such a waste."

"I know." He'd never in his life wanted to hold someone the way he wanted to hold her right that moment. Close to his heart, protected by his arms. "We need the police and an ambulance," he said gently.

She nodded woodenly and turned away.

LILY WALKED BACK into the police interrogation room and slipped her phone into her purse. "Gerard and Kinsey will be here tomorrow to take Charlie back to the ranch."

"I think Seth will actually be sad to see him leave," Chance said.

The police detective returned to the room, as well. "This is what's happening, folks," he said as he sat down opposite them. "First of all, Boise police knew all along that the man who confessed and subsequently killed himself wasn't the murderer. They say they were close on the heels of the truth and they appreciate the information you'll be able to share. Secondly, since you aren't pressing kidnapping charges against the Brightons and seeing as Betsy Connor confirms your story of what happened in the basement, you can go. However, there's a federal prosecutor bringing Jimmy's remains up here tomorrow and he wants to talk to you about your evidence against DA Block. We'd appreciate it if you stuck around Greenville for a couple more days."

"Of course," replied Chance. "We're at the inn down the street."

"I guess burying Jimmy at White Cliff is as close to a happy ending as Elizabeth is going to get," Lily said.

Chance reached for her hand. "I think so. There are a lot of victims here because of Tabitha and Jeremy. I'm just thankful you and Charlie aren't two of them."

She squeezed his hand and nodded. "Or you," she whispered.

Kinsey and Gerard met them the next day at the inn. The White Cliff/Greenville tragedies were still headlining news stories, not just in Greenville, but all across the country. The mixture of teenage sex, violence and survivalist upbringing made for juicy tabloid reporting that Lily did her best to shield Charlie from seeing. Buried in the back pages was the story that interested her more: the disappearance of what appeared to be the corrupt DA of Boise, Jeremy Block.

"I can't believe he's just disappeared," Kinsey commented as she packed Charlie's gear into the back of Gerard's car.

"I just wish they'd caught him," Lily said as she buckled her son into the car seat she'd bought for his journey back to Hastings Ridge.

"I bet you'd give anything to visit him behind bars," Kinsey added.

Lily did her best to return Kinsey's smile, but the worry of not knowing exactly where Jeremy was wouldn't go away. She'd heard he'd crossed into Canada and fervently hoped he just kept going.

Kinsey spontaneously hugged her as though she could tell what Lily was thinking. Maybe she could. They'd become close the summer before and that friendship now promised to grow even stronger.

"Thanks for taking Charlie back with you to the ranch," Lily said. "We'll be there as soon as we can."

BY THE TIME Chance drove the old truck over the cattle guard onto Hastings Ridge land, they were ready to enjoy a reprieve from media attention. Days of law offices and police stations had exhausted them both. Officials had agreed to give them a couple of days to settle things at the ranch before coming back to Boise where the ongoing investigation into the DA office and Jeremy Block's corruption needed information only Lily could provide.

That meant they'd be back in the thick of things very soon, but for now they were home.

"I placed you and your family in jeopardy when I was here last summer," Lily murmured as they drove down the gravel road. The first snow of the season had flown but it was only a light dusting. The black cattle in the fields stood out against the newly white earth and Chance felt a part of himself kind of thaw.

He put his hand over hers. "Don't think of it that way. There isn't a person here who doesn't love you both."

"We should have called and told them we were coming home a day early," she said.

"You wanted to surprise Charlie, remember?"

"Yes, but now it seems silly. I should have at least warned Grace or Kinsey that we'd be here at dinnertime."

"You're forgetting, Lily. There's always enough food on that table to feed everyone for about three days. Stop worrying."

"I'm trying," she said. "It just seems impossible we're finally nearing the end of this ordeal. I'll feel better when

Jeremy is caught but I bet you a million dollars he's on the other side of the world by now. The man is a survivor. Kind of like a cockroach."

"You're a survivor, too," Chance assured her. "Look, we're almost there," he added as they crested the hill and caught a glimpse of the ranch house below.

The main house and a few outbuildings were nestled on a large promontory created by a U-bend in the river that snaked through Hastings land. Wooded acreage rose up the slope north of the house, land that eventually reached a huge plateau complete with splendid examples of spreading oak trees that had been standing for decades. Past the plateau, an old mining ghost town quietly crumbled to the earth. The town had seen its share of tragedy, both in the past and more recently when Gerard's former family met untimely deaths by falling through a floor.

South of the house, the road followed the river, ending at last at Gerard's house which he now shared with his fiancée, Kinsey. They had passed Chance's own A-frame cabin a mile or two back while Pike was in the middle of constructing a home for himself north of the ranch house. Frankie, the youngest brother, still bunked at the main house. Well, he did when he was home, which wasn't a whole lot.

Daylight this late in the year disappeared comparatively early and so now, at twilight, the house was brightly lit and a curl of gray smoke rose into the sky. Chance drove down the road and circled back next to the house, parking in the area set aside for that purpose. The headlamps swept the porch as he turned and they saw the back door burst open and a small figure dash outside accompanied by three smaller shapes—the dogs.

As soon as the truck stopped, Lily opened her door

and jumped to the ground. Chance got out of the truck, but stopped short of advancing, wanting to give Lily the space he instinctively felt she needed. Charlie flew into his mother's arms. She twirled him around while the dogs barked and ran after their own tails.

Lily finally stopped spinning and just hugged Charlie until he slipped back to the ground and ran back into the house. She looked across the yard and apparently saw him leaning against the truck. Stretching out her hand, she smiled and he went to join her.

Chapter Twelve

Phone calls were made and people started to gather. By the time Grace set a roast on the large trestle table, everyone had heard the latest news and welcomed Lily and Charlie "home." They all acted like she belonged there with them and it was hard not to buy into all this goodwill. Did Chance find their acceptance of her threatening? She couldn't tell for sure. He was sensitive enough to her feelings by now that she knew he wouldn't go out of his way to hurt her, but she wasn't interested in trapping him, either.

She looked across the table and met Kinsey's gaze.

"I'm riding out to the ghost town tomorrow," Kinsey said. "I want to sketch. Do you want to come with me?"

"I'd love to watch you draw," Lily said. "Call me in the morning. It'll kind of depend on how Charlie does."

Chance had obviously overheard this conversation. "I'd be happy to take Charlie on an easier ride tomorrow to check out the cattle Gerard and Pike brought down from the hills."

"Do you think he's capable of that?" Lily asked.

"With help, sure."

Frankie had actually joined them for dinner and he sat down next to Kinsey and smiled at Lily. Since all of the

Hastings brothers had individual mothers, there were differences in their appearances and to a large extent, their temperaments. Chance could be a mischief-maker and a flirt, but Frankie had something else going on, as well. There was a darker side to him. He'd spent most of his youth in and out of trouble with the law, chosen friends poorly and tried everyone's patience. Lily didn't know him as well as she knew the others, but the one and only time they'd had a private conversation, he'd admitted he knew he'd been labeled the black sheep of the family and that was fine with him.

As far as looks went, he carried his share of the Hastings gene pool very well. He'd be thirty next year and while he looked friendly enough most of the time, there was also an experienced, tested quality to his eyes. His hair was lighter than Chance's or Gerard's, almost blond in the summer, darker now that fall had arrived with winter nipping at its heels. He sat next to Charlie who adored Frankie.

At the head of the table, Harry Hastings, the patriarch of the family, held rule, but he looked a lot more relaxed than he had the last time Lily had seen him. Then he'd just returned from his honeymoon and summer was in full swing. He'd had a lot on his mind. Tonight he looked almost cheerful, and he smiled often.

When dinner was over, Chance announced that Lily and Charlie would be staying with him at the A-frame. Lily had made this decision when Chance revealed his house was off the main road and few people knew about it. It seemed like a nice refuge and that's what she wanted right now—refuge.

And, to be honest, time with Chance. There were issues to settle.

"But Mommy, I don't want to go," Charlie said.

Frankie ruffled Charlie's hair. "We'll do it next week, sport, don't worry."

"Do what?" Lily asked.

Pike explained. "Frankie and Charlie and me had planned to spend tonight in a tent."

"But it's cold outside," Lily said.

"Inside the house, Mommy," Charlie said with a grin. "We're going to roast marshmallows and sing campfire songs and Uncle Frankie is going to tell me a scary story about the hanging tree."

The hanging tree was called that for a reason. Four bank robbers had made off with the town's payroll decades before. Three had been caught and hung while the money and the fourth man had disappeared forever. The story went that the dead men were left to rot at the end of their ropes because no one cut them down. Lily cocked an eyebrow at Frankie and said, "You're telling him what exactly?"

"A watered-down version," he whispered.

"The campfire is the fireplace," Pike added. "Sorry about getting the little guy's hopes up, we just didn't expect you home until tomorrow."

"Grandpa Harry said the dogs could sleep in the tent with us," Charlie whined. "Please, Mommy!"

"It must be a pretty big tent," Lily said.

"Not big enough," Pike said as an aside. "I've got my sights fixed on the sofa." He took off his glasses. There was a new look in his eyes, one Lily hadn't seen before. She touched his arm. "Is everything all right, Pike?"

"Just fine," he said quickly.

"Please, Mommy," Charlie said as he tugged on Lily's hand. "Can't I sleep in the tent? Just for tonight. Please?"

Lily looked at Chance who shrugged those impossibly broad shoulders. She looked at Pike and Frankie, two men she knew would protect Charlie no matter what the cost. Besides, he'd been here with them for two days already. "Sure," she finally said. "Of course."

"Okay, sport," Frankie said. "Let's set up the tent."

Lily looked from one man to the other. "Good luck, you guys. You know where I am if you need me."

She watched Charlie trot off with the two men, smiling to herself. It was going to be gut-wrenching taking him away from here, though she knew eventually that was going to happen. But maybe she could find a job in town and a little place for them to live where Charlie could still visit occasionally.

"Ready?" Chance called.

"I want to help Grace and Kinsey with the dishes…"

"Not tonight," Grace said as she walked past with a stack of plates. "Tonight, Gerard and Harry are washing, Kinsey and I are drying. Shoo."

After climbing back into the truck, Chance sat there for a second and stared at her. "What?" she asked. "Is something wrong?"

"I'm just surprised," he said.

"At what?"

"At you. I'm surprised you've agreed to come spend the night at my place without Charlie or anyone else to ride shotgun."

"Do I need someone to ride shotgun?" she asked sweetly.

"Yes, as a matter of fact, you do," he said, and started the truck.

She was quiet for a few moments as he drove out of the yard and back up the road. "I thought it would give us a chance to talk," she finally said as he turned off on the winding road that she surmised would lead to his A-frame.

"It's funny," he mused. "We've had time since everything happened but we haven't mentioned what's between us even once."

"I couldn't handle it," she said.

"But you're ready to figure it out now?"

"Yep. Oh, is that your place? It's charming."

"Thanks to the automatic lights you can actually see it," he said. "Come on inside."

The house had the typical highly peaked roofs of an A-frame. She was surprised at how spacious it was inside. "There's a loft bedroom upstairs that I use," he said. "There are two more bedrooms on the main floor, but they aren't furnished yet."

She raised her eyebrows and he laughed. "I'm sleeping on the couch tonight. You get the loft. Would you like a brandy?"

"Sure," she said.

"I'll take your satchel upstairs first," he said. "Make yourself at home."

The kitchen was small but efficient, lacking only the homey touches that would come with time. The dining room consisted of a card table and two chairs. The living room was the most pulled together space with a white shag area carpet anchored by a dark leather sofa and two huge chairs. Two tall windows flanked a rock fireplace where wood was stacked in preparation for a fire. Lily wandered over to one of the windows. The automatic outdoor lights had switched off, and as she stood in front of the black glass, backlit by the room behind her, she was suddenly aware of how visible a target she must make and backed away from the window, shivering now. She ran into Chance who lifted the snifters up high to avoid spilling their contents.

"Something spook you?" he asked.

"No," she said. She took the brandy he offered, clinked glasses, and took a sip. The fire burning down her throat helped clear her mind and chase away the boogie-man.

"Sit down," he said, patting the sofa seat next to him. Lily set her glass down on a small table.

"This is a comfortable house."

"Do you want me to start a fire?"

"That would be nice," she said, and scrunched back on the sofa while he fussed with paper and matches. For a second, she imagined Charlie back at the main house, toasting marshmallows and sleeping with the ranch dogs. A smile just got broader when Chance returned to the sofa. There was no denying the magnetism between them.

"Your face is back to normal," he said, raising a hand to lay his fingers against her cheek. "How come you've never been in my house before?"

"You never asked me."

"That's not true," he said. "The night we kissed, remember that night?"

"I remember."

"I asked you before the fateful kiss. You said you didn't think it would be a good idea."

"I did. Hmm," she said, and sipped more brandy.

"I have another theory," he added. "I think you didn't want to take the chance you might find a place you didn't want to leave."

"Your ego is one of your more endearing characteristics," she said with a soft chuckle. "That's why I thought you were like Jeremy when I first met you. You were just so sure of yourself, so positive a woman would be willing to settle for whatever you cared to offer."

"Comparing me to that psychopath is hitting beneath the belt," he grumbled.

She set aside her glass again. "But then I got to know you."

"And you discovered how dashing I am," he said.

"No, the dashing part was easy to see. What I found out is that you are a very good man."

"Don't go spreading that around," he said. "I have a reputation to protect."

She pretended to zip her lips, and they just both kind of mutually sank lower on the cushions, legs stretched out in front of them on an ottoman, the fire crackling and throwing wild shapes about the room.

"There's something I've been asking myself for a long time now," he said at last. She turned her head to find him looking right at her. He was so close she could feel his breath warm her skin. "I've been wondering and wondering what it is about you. Why do I crave you? Sure, you're gorgeous and interesting and sexy as hell, but frankly, lots of people are those things, right?"

She laughed internally. He sounded as though he was really struggling with this concept. She murmured, "Yes, right, lots of people."

He took her hand in his and squeezed it. "But I can't get past wanting you."

"And that's a problem for you?"

"Yes. You're not easy."

This time the laugh escaped her lips. "I know I'm not." She scooted even closer and his arm slipped around her back. She laid her head against his chest and sighed. "If it makes you feel any less alone in this endeavor, I find you just as hard to resist."

"And yet you do," he said softly.

"I've been running and hiding for so many years, first from myself, then Jeremy… I've just forgotten how to trust people. I'm trying, but I keep feeling any moment now, I'm going to have to grab Charlie and head for the hills."

"I know you do."

She raised her chin and looked up at him, stretched a little more and touched his lips with hers. "But there's this thing between us," she whispered. "Maybe it is just lust. Maybe what we have is supposed to be like a storm, you know, crazy and wild and then over." She looked up into his eyes. "It would be easier if I left and you forgot I ever existed."

"Maybe," he said. "But that's not going to happen and you know it. I've been thinking about no one else but you since the moment I saw you standing in the yard with your wild chopped blond hair and dangling earrings catching the light like sparklers. I admit it, I rushed you, I was crazy to have you. I would have said or done almost anything to get through to you."

"What makes you think you didn't get through to me?"

"You ran off when I kissed you."

"That wasn't just a kiss and you know it," she said. "With you it's never just a kiss." She was about to expound on this theory when he pulled her against him and proved what she'd just said. He kissed her so deeply that it was like the warm mouth of heaven opened to claim her. He teased her tongue with his and she held onto him tighter, pressing against him, the simmering heat off his skin musky and corporeal. His kisses went deep, lasted long, the storm she'd predicted hovering on the horizon about to shake the earth with thunder.

He stood up abruptly and pulled her to her feet. Then he leaned down and lifted her into his arms.

"What are you doing?" she asked breathlessly.

"I'm taking you to bed."

"Just like that?"

"Just like what? I'm been thinking of doing nothing else since last February. However, we're in no rush, and contrary to what you think of me, I'm not going to simply have my way with you." He carried her up the stairs to the bedroom and deposited her on the bed. Then he stared down at her. "You look disappointed," he said as he pulled off his shirt. "Did you just assume I was going to run amok on your naked body?"

She gazed at his bare chest and bit her lip. "I guess I did. However, if that's not your plan, why are you undressing? I thought you were going to sleep on the couch."

"Can't you stop thinking about sex for thirty seconds?" he teased. "I'm getting ready for bed is all. This is my room, after all." He sat down beside her. "You know what you are, Lily Kirk?"

She lowered her head and kissed his chest, then ran a hand downward. He picked up her hand and held it.

"No, what am I?"

"Spoiled. You've gotten so used to me wanting you—"

She put her finger across his lips. "Just shut up and kiss me, will you please?"

"Not so fast," he said. He took off his boots and socks, then stood. "You might want to stop gawking at me," he said. "The jeans are coming off next."

"I'll gawk, thanks," she said and admired the muscles rippling under the skin in his back and shoulders as he unbuttoned his jeans and took them off. Then he spread his arms. "Like what you see?"

She rotated her finger in the air and he did a 360, a silly grin plastered on his face. She could see what this bantering was doing to his anatomy—a guy had a hard time hiding certain things about himself—and it thrilled her.

"Your turn," he said and sat down again. She stood up and unbuttoned her sweater, then pulled off her shirt. He produced a wolf whistle and she bowed from the waist.

"Thank you," she said.

His expression softened as he crooked a finger. "Come here. That bra looks tricky. You may need help getting it off." She stepped closer to him, trembling as he ran his fingers across the bra, feeling his quickening breath clear down in her groin as her breasts escaped the delicate lingerie. She slipped off her jeans, leaned forward and kissed him then put her knee between his legs and pushed him back on the bed, climbing up to join him, straddling him.

His gentle caresses grew more intense as his warm mouth seemed to devour her. He pulled her hips against his. His engorgement between her legs drove her mad and she lay down on top of him, anxious for her bare breasts to touch his chest. He kissed her again and again until there was no definition, until he rolled her over onto her back and stared down into her eyes. His gaze seemed to burn through her skin.

He slowly lowered his head and kissed her, sucking gently on her lower lip. Everything changed. There was no stopping, no going back, no second thoughts. This is what they had both wanted since laying eyes on each other, an abandoned romp where thoughts were as unnecessary as clothes, where bare skin and hot moistness met urgency, where need, exhilarated by desire, pushed them to the breaking point.

There was nothing shy about Lily's investigation of Chance's magnificent physique. The skin on his butt was amazingly smooth and soft, and to possess even temporary power to arouse him to the point he could no longer delay plunging himself into her body was a mystifying feeling.

For an hour or more, they loved each other with abandon. He was a generous lover, rough when it aroused her, gentle when she asked for it, tireless in pleasing her just as she pleased him. Lily had only slept with one other man in her life and he'd boasted he felt about sex the same way he felt about almost every aspect of life: he was in it to win it. Sex hadn't been about desire followed by tenderness. For Jeremy, it had been about conquest, about planting a flag and moving on, not raining tender kisses over a lover's breasts and belly and beyond.

Chance erased that past. And later, when he held her in his arms and drifted off to sleep, she comforted herself that even if she never slept with him again, or more likely, they slept together often until their differences drove them apart, well, even if that happened, she had this moment.

It would be foolish to put too much meaning into what had happened that night. She just had to try to go with the flow and keep her head and give him the room to bolt when the time came.

CHANCE AWOKE WITH a start. He opened his eyes and found Lily sound asleep beside him. She was still here! His lips curved. There was a time not so long ago that last night's sex would have sated his hunger for her and maybe in the back of his mind, he was hoping that was still a possibility. He could tell himself that sex wouldn't change the nature of their relationship; experience had told him that wasn't true. What usually happened was a moment of bliss followed by trepidation as he pondered how to slip away into the night.

For the first time in his life he didn't want to slip away. He wanted the silken bonds he could feel entwining his body and heart to grow stronger. Last night, the more she'd responded to him, the more he'd wanted to give her. The feeling persisted even now. He wanted her here, in this bed, in this house, on this ranch. The thought she and Charlie could disappear again terrified him.

He kissed her cheek and her lashes fluttered. Damn if he didn't find it sexy. "Time to face the day," he whispered. Her phone rang and she groaned. He found her jeans on the floor and tugged the phone out of the pocket. "Looks like it's Kinsey," he said, adding, "Your phone is almost dead. There's a hookup over there on the desk."

Lily sat up straight and smiled at him as the sheet fell around her waist. Naked and tousled, she looked good enough to coax under the sheets for another hour or two. He handed her the phone, sighed, and went to take a shower.

Things got off to a slower start than they'd anticipated when they found the horses had somehow escaped their pasture and wandered off here and there across the fields. Chance finally cornered Jangles, his gorgeous bay gelding, and helped Lily saddle him. That had taken a while as it had been peppered with longing looks between Lily and Chance and excited babble from Charlie detailing the events of the living room campout.

An hour later, she and Kinsey rode past the hanging tree on their way to the ghost town. The October morning was cold and crisp and the snowy ice that had fallen the day before crackled beneath the horses' feet.

"Do you have any idea what you want to draw?" Lily asked Kinsey as they rode abreast.

"Not really. I like to stay open to inspiration. I won't do anything with the building where Gerard lost his family," she said. "I just want to take a look and see what attracts my attention. I hope it won't be boring for you."

"It won't. I've been wanting to investigate the place myself before it's nothing but a heap of wood."

"Just be careful," Kinsey warned.

"I will."

Kinsey studied her for a second and smiled. "You're different today."

"I am?"

"Yeah. You didn't snap at Chance once this morning."

Lily shrugged. "He's not so bad." She slid Kinsey a sidelong glance and added, "As a matter of fact, he's pretty spectacular."

"I knew it!" Kinsey said. She wore a bright yellow baseball hat that had once belonged to Gerard. That and the backpack strapped to her coat made her look like a college student riding to a class. "Finally," she added with an exaggerated sigh.

"Finally. Speaking of Hastings men, what's going on with Pike? He seemed a little distant last night. Chance said he's worried about his sister?"

"Tess isn't really his sister," Kinsey said. "Pike's mom and Tess's dad got together about twelve years ago which in that neck of the woods make theirs a long standing relationship. Heck, I guess it does almost anywhere anymore. Anyway, he was the star of that television show that only aired one season, the one about a private eye married to a belly dancer."

"I'm not big on TV," Lily admitted.

"It was on a long time ago. Rumor has it he got booted when he went into rehab. Tess was born about then and eventually came to live with him. I guess he cleaned himself up. He does television ads and voiceovers now and someone said he bought a restaurant or something. Anyway, Pike has never lived in the same house with Tess but he seems very protective of her. She left when Mona kicked her dad out of the mansion, but no one has heard a word from her since."

"There's always someone or something to worry about," Lily mused.

"Are you worried about Jeremy?"

Lily thought back to the shiver she'd experienced when she stood framed in Chance's window the night before. But Jeremy was in Canada or beyond, it was just the last of her overburdened nervous system working out the kinks. "Not really," she said, and squeezing her knees, urged her horse into a trot. "Last one there is a rotten egg," she called over her shoulder.

They slowed down when the first building rose to their left. The main street stretched out ahead, overgrown with weeds, flanked with buildings slowly sagging to the earth. Lily soon became distracted by an old saloon complete with a decayed-looking balcony. They dismounted and draped the reins over the remains of a hitching post. Kinsey untied a roll from the back of the saddle and produced a folding stool where she perched to open her backpack and withdraw the sketch pad and charcoal pencils. Lily looked over her shoulder for a while, amazed at how adroit her friend was at capturing the nuances of light and shadow. Eventually, she wandered down the street alone, quickly caught in the mystery of the past, wishing Chance was by her side, holding her hand.

GERARD RODE OUT with Chance and Charlie to look at the last herd of cattle brought down from the mountains. With Charlie riding in front of him in the saddle, he took it slow. Charlie, meanwhile, played with the palomino's mane and hummed a tune Chance recognized. Undoubtedly, Frankie had been whistling it the night before around the "campfire." The tune was catchy but the lyrics were borderline obscene and Chance hoped his brother hadn't shared those.

This group of Angus cattle would give birth for the first time this spring. For now it was important they grazed good fields. The cattle milled around the fence, looking for handouts, curious about the people staring at them while Charlie babbled on and on about dressing up as a cowboy for Halloween.

"Can I carry a gun?" he asked Chance.

"A real gun?"

"Yes."

"No."

"Please?"

"No, but we can make a pretend gun out of wood in the shop this afternoon. Would that do?"

"Yes!" Charlie cried and ran to the fence to tell the cows his big plan.

"He's a great kid," Gerard said.

"You bet he is," Chance agreed. "He's been through

a lot but he seems hardwired for happiness, especially when he's here."

"And you and Lily seem to have reached a new level in your relationship," Gerard added.

"You can tell?"

"Duh," Gerard said. "There's still tension between you two, but the nature of it is different. You, little brother, actually seem to be in love. I never thought I'd live to see the day."

Chance shook his head. "Too early to call it that," he grumbled but wasn't positive Gerard hadn't hit the nail on the head.

How did he feel about that? Scared, worried, trapped? Excited? Anxious?

Anxious was as good a word as any, he decided.

His cell phone rang and he was glad for the interruption from his head games. The area code was the one for Greenville but he didn't recognize the number. It was probably the police asking another question as they fought to build their case against Tabitha Stevens.

"Hello," he said, hoping this wouldn't take too long. Then he paused and listened. Meeting Gerard's glance, he finally spoke again into the phone. "Yes," he said. "I understand. Thanks."

"What—" Gerard started to say, but Chance shook his head.

"Lily's phone is at my house charging," he said. "Try calling Kinsey. Now."

Chapter Thirteen

Lily wandered the empty street, pausing to peer into some of the more intact-looking buildings. She didn't actually go into any of them as they were well posted with warning signs. The place could never be reclaimed. It was just a matter of time before the Hastings family would have to demolish it or risk further accidents.

Eventually she ended up at the end of town where the old mining site had existed a long, long time ago. A few pieces of rusted equipment and boards barring entry into the cave itself were all that was left of a human presence. The cave reminded her of the tunnel back at White Cliff and she stared at it for a few minutes, lost in thought, reliving that long hike through the earthy darkness and the accompanying horror of not knowing where Charlie was.

But she knew where he was now. Chance would take care of him, Chance wouldn't let anything or anyone harm him. Charlie was safe, she was safe.

So why was she shivering?

Well, it was cold outside. The coat Chance had bought her was warm, but her cheeks stung from the breeze. She plunged her hands into her pockets and turned to retrace her steps, although she paused at the bank where the robbery signaled the beginning of the end of Falls Ridge.

It was difficult not to speculate about the man who got away with the money. Where did he go? Was he able to enjoy his ill-gotten goods or did the ghosts of his former colleagues haunt him to the end?

And who was he? As far as she knew, the other three men had been locals, but the fourth man was a mystery.

A mystery. Like Chance. What was he thinking? Was he ready to bolt? How could she ever bear seeing him lose interest in her, sensing his needs had been filled and he was ready to move on to a new adventure, a new lover?

Was he the reason she shivered inside? Was this haunting fear one of rejection?

She checked her watch and saw that it was time they started home. A few more minutes and she rounded a slight curve. Jangles and Kinsey's mount should be visible now, but they weren't. Had the horses wandered off? She picked up her pace to ask Kinsey what was going on. But Kinsey wasn't where Lily had left her. The stool rested on its side while the sketch pad lay on the ground, the top sheet fluttering in the biting wind. Charcoal pencils had scattered across the half-frozen earth. The small bag that held the rest of the art supplies sat exactly where it had when Lily last saw it. There were no footprints on the cold, hard-packed earth.

So, had the horses run off and had Kinsey left to get them back? Had the wind caught the sketch pad and blown it to the ground? Was that what pushed over the stool?

"Kinsey?" she called, and though her voice didn't echo, it did sound hollow and forlorn. She kept walking, looking into dark, open doorways as she passed, calling Kinsey's name as she went. Despite there being no evidence of foul play, it was hard to shake a growing feeling of foreboding and she quickened her pace.

She finally caught a glimpse of yellow coming from inside a heavily shadowed building. Was that Kinsey's hat? Lily knew Kinsey would never willingly go inside one of these old deathtraps. Lily stepped up onto the wooden sidewalk, avoided a cave-in and entered the building. She plucked the yellow cap from the floor and scanned the empty room.

The only standing fixture was a counter along one wall. She leaned over it and found Kinsey on the floor. After rushing to her side, she knelt by her friend's body and felt for a pulse in her throat. When Kinsey's heartbeat leapt to greet her touch, Lily swallowed a sob of relief.

A red mark on Kinsey's head suggested she'd been hit. Who had done this to her and why?

How could it be Jeremy but how could it not? Her mind refused to leap farther than him, but it didn't make sense. He was in Canada. She searched Kinsey's pockets for her cell phone but couldn't find it. She had to get help. She had to know what happened. Maybe the phone was in the backpack with the art supplies still resting by the stool. She lifted Kinsey's shoulders, determined to drag her out of this building, but that wasn't as easy as it sounded.

Kinsey's eyes opened. "Gerard?" she mumbled.

"No, sweetie, it's me, Lily. Thank goodness you're awake. Can you stand up? We have to get you out of here."

"Gerard," Kinsey repeated. "Gerard…"

Lily relaxed her hold on the other woman's shoulders. "It's okay," she said, smoothing her hair. "I'll get help."

"…baby," Kinsey whispered as her eyes closed again.

Was she talking about Gerard or was it possible Kinsey was pregnant? Oh, God, if she died in this town carrying Gerard's baby the poor guy would never recover. Lily took off her coat and tucked it around Kinsey's still form, then she leaned over her and listened to the sound of her breathing. It seemed steady enough.

One way or another, she had to summon aid and the best bet for that was to find Kinsey's cell phone. She ran outside and started back toward the saloon, her gaze darting everywhere. Someone had hurt Kinsey. That someone was probably still around and there were so many places to hide…

Suddenly a man detached himself from the shadows of a covered sidewalk and stepped onto the street about a hundred feet away. "Lily," he said in a voice that still struck terror in her heart.

She turned around and took off, the sound of his laughter ringing out behind her. "Run if you want. Where are you going to go?"

Good question, but for now all she wanted was distance and her feet hit the ground with only that in mind. She looked back over her shoulder and saw that Jeremy had started running after her. She passed the building where Kinsey lay, her only thought to get this monster away from her friend and to escape herself.

Of course it was Jeremy. Who else would it be? His stride was longer than hers and he jogged every day of his life. She knew she could not outrun him forever. She also knew she would leave the relative safety of the town very soon and be out in the open. Glimpsing an alley between two buildings, she sprinted to her right. This would take her back toward the saloon and the promise of the phone, but the alley was a dangerous place as it was too narrow to offer protection. Doors opened off it, doors that led into ramshackle structures, one more treacherous than the next. A blast from behind kicked up a puff of dirt to her left as Jeremy fired a gun at her, and she realized nothing inside those buildings could be more terrifying than what pursued her from behind.

She had to get that phone. She darted into a nondescript building and saw the door onto the street ahead of her. Sure enough, she exited a few feet from the overturned stool. She grabbed the backpack and ran into the saloon. There was no visible exit, in fact, most of the back wall had crumpled inside. Footsteps sounded outside and she took the only route open to her and that was the stairs. She stopped at the top and flattened herself against a wall as she heard the thud of Jeremy's footsteps grind to a halt below her.

"Lily!" he yelled.

She tried to quiet her breathing as she felt around the heavy pack stuffed with Kinsey's art supplies. Momentary joy turned to despair when what she thought was the phone turned out to be only a metal case for a small package of tissues. The phone wasn't in the backpack.

"I know you're here," he said. He wasn't even breathing hard. "We can do this easy or we can do this hard." She heard his footsteps as he approached the stairs.

She was terrified he would go back for Kinsey and try to use her as a hostage. She couldn't think of a single thing she could do to stop him. He was stronger, meaner, and he had a gun. But he also had something else, something she understood the power of: he had nothing to lose.

"You didn't think I'd stay in Canada without a fitting farewell to my lovely bride, did you?" he said. She could hear him moving around. What was he doing down there?

She looked around the darkened area in which she

stood. It appeared to be a hallway with doors spaced along it like the rooms of a small hotel. One door stood open and light from it spilled into the dark hall. She inched along the wall. The creaks her footsteps created seemed to jump through the building.

"Might as well come down here," he called.

She wanted to tell him to shut up, but maybe she should engage him in dialogue. The sound of their voices might mask her movement. "I'm not your bride," she hollered.

He laughed. "My first wife is dead now, Lily. That kind of makes you my one and only."

"Elizabeth's not dead," Lily yelled.

"Au contraire," he said. Lily heard something splinter or break downstairs. "I took her out yesterday morning. One shot, right between the eyes. Damn good aim if I do say so myself. I could have done the same exact thing to you. I mean, I had you in my sights last night and this morning, too. But you've really been a pain in the ass. I want to put my hands around your lovely little neck. I want you to look at me when I kill you. I want you to know your lying lover is next. I've already done his family, I just need to find him. But I will. He'll die after you and so will anyone else who gets between me and my kid."

She swallowed what felt like an iceberg. "What did you do to Chance's family?"

"Never you mind. You have your own troubles."

"Please, please, just leave. Don't hurt anyone else, don't take Charlie, you don't love him," she said, coming to a halt across the hall from the open door. "He'll slow you down. You're on the run now."

"I am not on the run," he said. "People like you run, Lily. People like me triumph."

She stopped moving when she got across from the illuminated room. For a second, she struggled with her emotions, tears perilously close to blurring her vision. But that was what Jeremy wanted and she would never again give him the satisfaction of breaking her. People she loved were depending on her. She would not let them down.

She focused on the room. Half the outer wall had disintegrated, showing nothing through the opening but gray skies. What kind of structure was next door? She inched her way toward the light.

Maybe she could use Jeremy's emotions against him. He had to have a raw nerve somewhere. "What about your other son?" she called out.

He didn't respond.

"You must have freaked out when Maria reported that you and Elizabeth had a son and that very son was sitting downtown in your jail, a confessed murderer. How would that look to the people you kiss up to? They would have distanced themselves from you. Your career would be over. I'm surprised you didn't kill the boy yourself."

"Who said I didn't?" he said.

She stopped short. "You murdered Jimmy? How? He hung himself. Besides, I saw you that night, you came home and took out your anger on me."

"That wasn't anger, dear-heart, that was a celebration. I gave him the rope," he added, "in a figurative way, that is. I told him I knew he was covering for someone. I promised him I would find out who it was and I would prosecute them and then pull the switch on the electric chair myself. I swore I would then go after his mother and every whacko in White Cliff. The kid almost wet himself he was so scared. He asked what he could do to fix things and I told him what I once told you."

"You told him it would be better off all around if he

was dead," she said, reliving for an instant the moment he'd said the same thing to her. No wonder the boy killed himself. She had never met Jimmy but her gut clenched as she imagined the pain he must have felt when his long-lost father told him to sacrifice his own life to save the lives of the people he loved. Jimmy had been Charlie's half brother and he was dead and now this jerk wanted to take Charlie. "You are a bastard," she yelled.

"Sticks and stones," he said. "Take a deep breath, Lily. Do you smell something?"

She had inched her way into the room and now approached the crumbled wall. She couldn't allow Jeremy to take Charlie. She had to do something. The roof of the building next door was six feet away with a drop of about the same. The roof had caved in in one place. She might possibly survive a jump but would her weight and momentum send her crashing down through layers of rotting wood?

And then Jeremy's last comment finally sank into her brain. She crept back toward the hall and sniffed the air—smoke!

"The flames are almost touching the stairs," Jeremy called. "Unless you want to burn to death, you better come on down and take your chances with me. I wouldn't wait too long to make up your mind."

Smoke was seeping through the boards by her feet, drawn to the open wall behind her. If she went downstairs he would shoot or strangle her. If she jumped out that window, she chanced injury or death.

She turned around, gripped Kinsey's backpack in front of her to provide some cushion between her bones and the roof, ran toward the opening and jumped. She hit the neighboring building with a crash and lay very still for a few seconds, not sure if she was just winded from the fall or hurt more badly, taking shallow breaths to control the pain and afraid to move lest the roof give in. Her leg throbbed and her hands burned.

The smell of smoke was more pronounced. A fire in this dead town would move quickly, leaping from roof to roof until there was nothing left but ashes. Kinsey was unconscious less than a block away and no one knew she was there but Lily. Somehow she had to recover enough to get off this roof, evade Jeremy and drag Kinsey out of that building.

Sensing movement, she struggled into a sitting position in time to witness Jeremy launch himself from the opening through which smoke now billowed. He landed a few feet away from her and immediately started to stand, but the stress of his impact following hers was too much for the old roof and it groaned like a tortured ghost. As Jeremy pulled the gun from his waistband, the roof cracked one last time and gave way. Lily fell downward with the wreckage, gripping the raw wood beneath her to keep from sliding into free fall.

Her sitting position helped her maintain some balance and she landed on top of a heap of rubble, jarred to the bone. Debris rained down on her head and the smell of smoke was already creeping into the building. She glanced upward and saw ragged beams torn from the walls and roof, some swinging precariously.

She turned to look for Jeremy. Caught in motion when the roof gave way, he hadn't fared as well as she had and had landed farther down the pile of rubble. He lay facedown, his left arm twisted at a terrible angle. Even as she stared, he somehow got to his feet and lifted the gun with his right hand. The barrel pointed straight at her chest.

Lily realized she still clutched the backpack. She heaved it forward as hard as she could, her strength and aim sharpened by desperation. At the same moment the pack hit the top of his head, the gun exploded, deafening her. She fell onto her bottom and slid downward, grasping for something to stop her descent, finally coming to a halt when a jutting board caught her in the chest. For a second she sat there winded again, eyes closed, trying to breathe, waiting for searing pain to announce where Jeremy's bullet had struck her. Pain didn't come.

She opened her eyes. There was no sign of the backpack but Jeremy lay nearby, on his back, staring upward at flames licking the edges of what was left of the roof. She didn't see his gun anywhere but she fully expected him to rally yet again.

And then she saw the blood spurting from his neck where a nail-studded board had apparently fallen from the rafters, pinning him down and puncturing his carotid artery. She scrambled toward him on stinging hands and skinned knees. The glancing impact of the backpack must have knocked him off his feet. Maybe a reflex action of his trigger finger fired the gun and maybe the bullet dislodged the rafter that subsequently fell, impaling him.

He blinked and she realized he was still alive. Half afraid the geyser of blood was really a trick of some kind, she moved even closer. Thoughts of smoke and mirrors vanished as she watched the color drain from his skin, shrinking him before her eyes. She knelt beside him. The edge of a handkerchief stuck out of his pocket and she grabbed it. Kinsey's phone tumbled out with the cloth. Lily held the handkerchief against his neck without touching the horrid board, without hearing the fire overhead or feeling the warmth of his blood splattering against her arm. The contact of the cloth seemed to signal his dying brain that he wasn't alone. His focus shifted to her face for the briefest of seconds, recognition dawned in his eyes and then he looked straight through her into oblivion.

"Lily!"

She jerked. The action slid her against Jeremy. Repulsed, she stood on wobbly legs as Chance and Gerard ran into the building. Both men stopped suddenly as their gazes traveled from the dead man, up to her face and then to the roof.

"Look out!" Gerard yelled.

Lily glanced upward and saw a burning board teetering over her head. Caught in some kind of limbo, she saw sparks fly across the sky. The next thing she knew, Chance was beside her. He threw her over his shoulder and scrambled down the pile before shifting her weight into his arms and handing her down to Gerard who asked if she could stand. She nodded. Chance jumped to the ground and grabbed one of her arms. Gerard took the other. It felt to Lily like she flew out of there on the wings of two guardian angels. A crash from behind announced the rest of the ceiling had tumbled into the building.

Her feet finally hit the dirt of Main Street. Chance grabbed her arms and searched her face. "Are you okay? You're covered with blood. Where are you hurt?"

"It's Jeremy's blood," she said breathlessly. "You have to find Kinsey. She's in a nearby building. It's on the right side of the street as you come into town, the store with a long counter running along the back wall. You have to go save her."

"Sounds like the old mercantile," Chance said, glancing at Gerard who was already running down the street.

Lily looked back at Chance to find him studying her hands, which she was surprised to see were torn and bleeding from abrasions and imbedded splinters. No wonder they hurt. Pain was good, though. Pain meant she'd survived despite all the odds, despite Jeremy's pathological desire to erase her from the earth, despite her own misjudgments.

Chance kissed her wrist. "Oh, my darling, darling girl," he whispered, and met her gaze. There were tears in his eyes. She'd never been so happy to see anyone as she was him but that wasn't true, she'd felt this same way when she found Charlie in Maria's car. "Where's my child?" she asked.

"He's with my father."

"I'm so relieved to hear that. Jeremy insinuated he killed your family before he hit Kinsey and shooed away our horses."

"He was playing head games with you," Chance said.

"It might have worked if it hadn't been for Charlie and Kinsey…and you."

"You need to see a doctor," he said.

"I need you," she responded. "And Charlie and a pair of tweezers and some bandages."

"What happened to Block?"

"I'll tell you the long story later. The short version is he did his best to kill me but caused his own death instead. I might have contributed to that conclusion."

"That's my girl," he said, and raising her chin, kissed her lips.

She'd been fighting loving him for over nine months, leery of caring more than he did, of being hurt, of losing him because she gave herself to him, not just with her body, but with her heart. And all that meant was that she'd been running, yet again, but from herself this time…from the truth,

And she was done. The truth was she loved him. The truth was she needed him. He could accept those truths or not, his response couldn't change the way she felt, the way she would always feel about him.

Chance's and Gerard's horses were skittish because of the increasing smoke and danced around as Chance led them down the street. Lily took her first real breath of relief as Gerard helped Kinsey walk out of the mercantile. The fact she was on her feet was amazing to Lily, and she felt tears of thankfulness sting behind her nose. Kinsey held out Lily's coat and Chance took it, draping it around Lily's shoulders.

Kinsey leaned close to Lily. "Thank you," she said.

Lily produced a wry smile. "For almost getting you killed? Twice?"

"For helping me," she said. "For sending Gerard."

"Your baby," Lily whispered.

Kinsey smiled and touched her stomach area. "Don't tell Gerard, though. Not yet."

"That's your news to share," Lily said as her gaze traveled down the street to the flames tearing through the old wood. In a triumph of poetic justice, Jeremy's body burned in the inferno he'd created.

Chance called his dad who said he would err on the side of safety by topping off the tank in the water-hauling truck and driving the alternate route up to the plateau and across to the ghost town, just in case the winds shifted. He also said he would call the police and all four of them groaned as they anticipated the rash of questions to come.

There was no sign of the two horses Jeremy had released, but they did find a big roan tethered outside of town. "That's one of our mares," Gerard said, pausing to help Kinsey climb into the saddle.

"Block must have let the horses out of the field when he stole her," Chance said. "I never thought to check the tack and see if any of that was missing."

Gerard climbed onto his horse and Chance lifted Lily into the saddle and climbed behind her. There was no way she could handle reins with her injured hands but his arms provided all the stability she needed.

"I have to tell you some bad news," Chance said as they rode along. "Elizabeth was killed yesterday."

"I know about that. Jeremy bragged about shooting her through the forehead. But how did you know?"

"Seth Brighton called. His father had been trying to reach you since realizing the only one in the world who would shoot Elizabeth as she stood at the sink inside her own house staring out at all those dead sunflower plants was Jeremy Block. When he couldn't get ahold of you, he asked Seth to call me. Then Gerard tried to call Kinsey but she didn't answer."

"Jeremy took her phone," Lily said. "She was out cold in the mercantile."

"I died a thousand times between hearing that Block was on a murdering rampage and the moment I found you," Chance added.

"I know the feeling," she said, leaning her head against his chest. "When he told me he was going after you next, it was as if he nailed spikes into my heart."

Chance kissed the top of her head. "Just so you know, I'm not letting you out of my sight again."

She turned to look into his dark eyes. "You're not?"

"No. I'll marry you if I have to."

She frowned. "Don't do me any favors."

"I didn't mean it that way—"

"Then how did you mean it? I took care of myself pretty darn good back there."

"Sure you did. One more minute and you would have been buried under a ton of burning roof."

"Now just a minute. You act like I go around getting into trouble just so you have to rescue me."

"I wouldn't put it past you."

"There's that ego again—"

He put a finger against her lips. "Just shut up and kiss me, will you please?"

"Oh, what the hell," she said, and touched her lips to his.

* * * * *

Look for more books in Alice Sharpe's
THE BROTHERS OF HASTINGS RIDGE RANCH
in 2016!

Read on for a sneak preview of
LUCKY SHOT,
the third book in
THE MONTANA HAMILTONS
by New York Times *bestselling author*
B.J. Daniels

Max made a few calls to see what kind of interest there was in the photos of Senator Buckmaster Hamilton with his first wife, the back-from-the-dead Sarah Johnson Hamilton. There was always skepticism with something this big. But not one of the people he called told him to get lost.

"Where can you be reached?" they each asked in turn. "I'll have to get back to you… Is there any chance of getting an exclusive if these photographs…?" The questions came.

Not one to count his chickens before they hatched, Max still couldn't help feeling as if the money was already in his pocket. He could already taste the huge steak he planned to have as soon as he got Kat Hamilton to verify that the photos he'd taken were of her long-lost mother.

Then it was just a matter of waiting for the calls to start coming in and the bidding to begin. All he had to do was wait around until four for Kat.

He'd parked his pickup down the street, so he could watch the art gallery and see who came and went. A little after four, he spotted Kat Hamilton. She looked just as she had in her photo on her website. He watched her climb out of a newer model SUV, pull a large folder from the back and head across the street toward the gallery.

As he got out of his pickup, he admitted that he was flying by the seat of his pants. He wasn't sure how he was going to play this. He just hoped that the Max Malone charm didn't let him down. Passing a shop window, he caught his reflection and stopped to brush back his too-long hair. He really needed a haircut, and a shave wouldn't hurt either, he thought as he rubbed a palm along his bristled jaw.

Well, too late for any of that. He straightened his shirt, sniffed to make sure he didn't reek—after all, he'd spent the night sleeping under the stars in the back of his truck. He smelled like the great outdoors, and from what he could tell, Kat Hamilton might appreciate that. Most of her photographs he'd seen were taken in the great outdoors.

Still, he knew this wasn't going to be easy. Kat Hamilton wasn't just a rich, probably spoiled artist. She was a rich, probably spoiled artist whose daddy was running for president and whose birth mother was possibly unstable. He had no idea what it was going to take to get what he wanted from the unapproachable Kat Hamilton.

When he pushed into the gallery, the bell over the door chimed softly and both women turned in his direction. The gallery owner looked happy to see him. Kat? Not so much. He saw her take in his attire from his Western shirt to his worn jeans and boots. He'd left his straw cowboy hat in the truck, but his camera bag was slung over one shoulder.

"This is the man I was just telling you about," the shop owner said.

Kat's gray eyes seemed to bore into him as he sauntered toward her. Mistrust and something colder made her gaze appear hard as granite. She was dressed in an oversize sweater and loose jeans, that approach-at your-own-risk look welded on her face.

"Max Malone," he said, extending his hand. "I'm a huge fan of your work, but I'm sure you hear that all the time."

Her handshake was firm enough. Her steely gaze never warmed, just as it never left his. "Thank you." Her voice had an edge to it, a warning. *Tread carefully.*

"I was especially taken with your rain photo," he said, moving in that direction, hoping she would take the hint and follow.

"You should show him your latest ones you brought in today," the gallery owner said.

Kat didn't jump at that.

"Would you mind if I took a photo of this? I want to show it to my wife. This would be perfect for her office."

"That would be fine," Kat said, clearly not invested in his company. He was reminded that she came from a wealthy family. She didn't need to make money from her photographs.

He snapped the shot of her rain photo and then walked back to where he'd left her standing. Every line of her body language said she'd had enough of him. He felt as if he was chipping away at solid ice. Charm wasn't going to get what he wanted. He hoped he wouldn't be forced to buy one of her photographs. The prices were a little steep, and he doubted cash would warm her up.

He was tempted, though, to buy the one she'd taken of the pouring rain. There was something about the shot…

"I hate to even show you the photo I took," he said, stopping next to her to show her a scenery shot he'd taken on his camera while he'd been waiting for her to show up at the gallery.

She gave the photo a cursory glance and started to turn away when he flipped to the one he believed to be of her mother.

Kat Hamilton froze. Her gaze leaped from the camera to him. She took a step back, her gray eyes sparking with anger.

"I'm sorry," he said innocently, even though he felt a surge of pleasure to see some emotion in her face. "Is something wrong?"

"Who are you?" she demanded. "You're one of those reporters who have been camped outside the ranch like vultures for weeks."

That pretty well covered it, while at the same time confirming what he already knew. The photo was of Sarah Hamilton.

"I guess I don't have to ask you if the woman in the photo is your mother," he said as he put his camera away.

"Do you want me to call the police?" the shop owner asked as she stood wringing her hands.

"No, this man is leaving," Kat said, glaring poison darts at him. She looked shaken. Clearly, he'd caught her flat-footed with the photo.

"For what it's worth, I really do like your photos." With that he left. She hurled insults after him. Not that he didn't deserve them.

He was just doing his job. He doubted Kat Hamilton had ever had a real job. But even though he could and would defend his to the death, he was always sorry when innocent people got hurt.

It was debatable how innocent Sarah Hamilton was at

this point, though. Unfortunately, her daughters would pay the price for her notoriety.

MAX HAD PLANNED to drive back to Big Timber. But as he crossed Main Street, he realized that he was starving. His productiveness had left him ready to call it a day. Stopping at a hotel with a restaurant on the lower level, he decided he'd stay in Bozeman for the night. He was about to leave his camera bag and laptop in his pickup, but changed his mind.

He knew he was being paranoid, but just the thought of someone breaking into his pickup, and stealing them and the photos on them, made him take the equipment with him. Earlier at Big Timber Java, he'd put the photos on a thumb drive and stuck it in his pocket. Still, he didn't want to take any chances.

He'd just sat down in the restaurant after getting a room, when the calls began coming in. He let them go to voice mail. He'd go through them in his room later. If he seemed too anxious it would make him look as if he didn't have the goods. He'd just ordered the restaurant's largest T-bone steak with the trimmings when he saw a pretty brunette sitting alone at a table perusing a menu.

She looked around as if a little lost. They made eye contact. She smiled, then put down her menu and got up to walk over to him. "I know this is going to sound forward..." She bit her lower lip as if screwing up her courage. "I hate eating alone and I've had this amazing day." She stopped. "I'm sorry. I'm sure you'd prefer—"

"Have a seat. I've had a pretty amazing day myself."

All her nervousness seemed to evaporate. "Thank you. I've never done anything like that before. I'm not sure what came over me," she said as she took a seat across from him. "It's just that I noticed you were alone and I'm alone…"

The woman looked to be a few years younger than his thirty-five years. After the day he'd had, he was glad to have company to celebrate with him.

"Max Malone," he said, holding out his hand.

"Tammy Jones." Seeing what was going on, the waitress set up cutlery at the table and took her order.

Tammy explained that she was a retail buyer for a local department store. She was in town visiting from Seattle. "I'm only in town tonight. I normally don't invite myself to a stranger's table. But I'm tired of eating alone and today I got a great raise. I feel as if I just won the lottery."

He told her he was on vacation and just passing through town. He'd found when he told anyone that he was a reporter, it made them clam up, too nervous that they might end up in one of his articles.

"I saw your camera bag. So what all do you shoot?" she asked, leaning toward him with interest.

"Mostly scenic photos," he said. "It's just a hobby." He didn't want to talk about his job. Not tonight. He didn't want to jinx it.

Their meals came, and they talked about movies, books, food they loved and hated. It was pleasant, so he didn't mind having an after-dinner drink with her at the bar. She had a sweet, innocent face, which was strange because she reminded him a little of Kat Hamilton, sans the gray eyes. He kept thinking of those fog-veiled eyes. Kat was a woman who kept secrets bottled up, he thought.

"Am I losing you?" Tammy Jones asked, touching his hand.

"No." He gave her his best smile.

"You seemed a million miles away for a minute there."

"Nope." Just at the gallery across the street where he'd seen a light on in the back. Was Kat Hamilton still over there? She'd brought in new photos, if that large flat portfolio she'd been carrying was any indication. He wished now that he'd asked to see them before he'd gotten thrown out.

"I know it's awful, but I'm not ready to call it a night." She met his gaze with a shy one. "A drink in my room?"

How could he say no? They took the stairs to her room on the second floor.

What could one more drink hurt? With a feeling of euphoria as warm as summer sunshine, he reminded himself of the photos he would be selling tomorrow.

When he woke the next morning, he was lying in the alley behind the hotel. While he still had his wallet, his camera and laptop were gone.

AS HE STUMBLED through the stupor of whatever he'd been drugged with, Max tried to figure out who'd set him up. He knew why he'd been so stupid as to fall for it. He'd wanted someone to celebrate with last night. As much as he loved his job, he got lonely.

Now, though, he just wanted his camera and laptop and the photos on them back. Maybe Tammy Jones—if that had even been her real name—had just planned to pawn them for money. But he suspected that wasn't the case once he checked his wallet and found he had almost a hundred in cash that she hadn't bothered with.

His head cleared a little more after a large coffee at a drive-through. He put in a call to the department store where Tammy Jones said she worked as a buyer, hoping he was wrong. He was told no one by that name worked for the company, not in Bozeman, not in Seattle.

He groaned as he disconnected. Whoever the woman had been last night, she had only one agenda. She was after the photos.

But how did she even know about them? He'd made a lot of calls yesterday and quite a few people were aware that he had the shots. All the people he'd called, though, he'd worked with before and trusted them. That left... No way was that woman from the restaurant hired by the senator to steal the photos. If the future president had known about the photos he would have tried to buy them if not strong-arm him, Max was sure.

That left Kat Hamilton.

He drove back downtown. It was early enough that the gallery wasn't open yet, but the light was still on in the back. He parked on Main Street and walked down the alley. The rear entrance in the deserted alley had an old door and an even older lock. One little slip of his credit card, and he was inside, thankful for his misspent youth.

The first thing he saw was a sleeping bag in one corner of the back area with a battery-operated lamp next to it and a book lying facedown on the floor. The woman clearly didn't appreciate the spines of books.

He found Kat wearing a pair of oversize jeans and a different baggy sweater. Clearly, this must be the attire she preferred. But he thought about bottled up secrets. Was she hiding under all those clothes? She stood next to a counter in the framing room of the gallery, her back to him, lost in her work. "I want my camera and laptop back."

At the sound of his voice, she spun around, gray eyes wide as if startled but not necessarily surprised. If he'd had any doubt who'd set him up, he didn't any longer. She'd known she'd be seeing him again.

"I beg your pardon?" she asked haughtily.

He enunciated each word as he stepped toward her. "The woman you hired to steal my camera and laptop? Tell her I want them back along with the photos of your mother and—"

"I have no idea what you're talking about."

He laughed. "Did anyone ever mention that you're a terrible liar?"

She bristled and looked offended. "I don't lie. Nor do I like being accused of something I didn't do."

"Save it," he said before she could deny it again. "I show you a photograph of your mother, and hours later my camera and laptop are stolen and you have no idea what I'm talking about?"

Kat shrugged. "Maybe you should be more careful about who you hang out with." She turned her back to him as she resumed what she'd been doing. Or at least pretended to.

"Look. Someone is going to get a photo of your mother sooner or later. Why go to so much trouble?"

She turned to face him. "Exactly. If not you, then someone else will get her photo. Do you think I really care that you took a photo of my mother with plans to sell it to some sleazy rag? I didn't and I still don't. I've lived in a fishbowl my whole life. I've had people like you in my face with cameras since my father first ran for office. It comes with the territory. My mother is just another casualty."

He took off his hat and scratched the back of his neck as he considered whether or not she was lying. He'd been bluffing earlier. "I'm not buying it. I saw your expression when you recognized your mother in the photograph."

She sighed. "Think what you like."

"Let's talk about another woman, the one you set me up with last night."

Hand on one hip, she turned to study him openly for a moment. "What did this woman look like?"

He described her. "Don't pretend you don't know her."

"I know her *type*." She smiled, noticeably amused. "Come on, weren't you even a little suspicious when she hit on you? She did hit on you, right? That's what I thought, and you fell for it. Whoever set you up must know you."

Max laughed. Kat had lightened up, and he liked her sense of humor. "I'll have you know, women hit on me all the time."

She rolled her eyes. "Chalk this up as a learning experience and move on." She started to turn away again.

"You really don't think I'm going to let you get away with this, do you?"

She sighed and faced him once more. "What option do you have? Even if you had a shred of proof, it would be my word, the daughter of a senator, against your word, a…reporter."

Okay, now she was ticking him off. "I happen to like what I do, and it puts food on my table." He glanced at the photos she was working on. "Who keeps food on your table? I doubt your…hobby of taking pictures is your means of support." He cocked his head at her. "Then again, you don't need to stoop to having a real job, do you?"

KAT HAD KNOWN she would see Max Malone again after he'd ambushed her yesterday. He would want a story about her mother. He would use the photos he'd gotten to bargain with her. This wasn't her first rodeo.

But she hadn't expected him to come in the back way accusing her of stealing his camera and laptop with the photos of her mother. If she'd known how easy it would have been, she might have considered setting him up just for the fun of it, though.

No, she had expected him to come through the front door and make a scene once the gallery opened. She'd been prepared to threaten to call the police on him.

But he'd surprised her in more ways than one. Not many men did that. So she'd let him have his say, waiting to see what his game was. She'd even found the man somewhat amusing at first, but now he was starting to irritate her.

"I'll have you know I take care of myself."

"Is that right? You pay for that fancy SUV you drive?" He laughed. "I didn't think so. Now about my camera—"

"If you think I'm going to replace your camera— What are you doing?" she demanded as he pulled out his cell phone and keyed in three numbers. She'd planned to *threaten* to call the police, but she wouldn't have done it because she didn't want the hassle or the publicity.

"Calling the cops."

"They'll arrest you for breaking into the gallery." She heard the 911 operator answer. He was calling her bluff. He knew she didn't want the police involved.

"I'd like to report—"

"Fine," she snapped.

He said, "Sorry, my mistake," into the phone and pocketed it again. He eyed her, waiting.

"But I don't have your camera or your laptop."

He studied her for a long moment. "Okay, if you want to play it that way, then what do you have to offer me?"

he asked as he leaned against the counter where she'd been working.

She gritted her teeth. Hadn't she suspected that he hadn't really lost his camera or laptop and that he was playing her? She no longer found him amusing. It was time to call a halt to this.

"Even though I had nothing to do with the loss of your camera or laptop, I'll write you a check for new ones just to get rid of you."

He shook his head slowly, his gaze lingering on her long enough that she could feel heat color her cheeks. He made her feel naked, as if he could see her the way no one else could. "*My* camera, *my* laptop, *my* photos. That's the only deal on the table, unless you have something more to offer."

"I just offered you money!"

He shook his head, his gaze warm on her.

She felt her cheeks flush as she realized what he was suggesting. "I have *nothing* more to offer you."

He raised a brow, shoved off the counter and closed the distance between them. "Either I get my camera back, or you're going to have to make it up to me in another way." He was close, too close, but it wasn't fear he evoked. She could smell the scent of freshly showered soap on him. Her gaze went from his blue eyes to his lips and the slight smirk there. The man was so cocky, so arrogant, so sure of the effect he was having on her.

As he brushed his fingertips over her cheek, she felt a tingle before she slapped his hand away. "If you think I'm going to sleep with you—"

"I said something that I would like *better*," he said.

Better than sleeping with her? "You really are a bastard."

He shook his head. "Untrue. Both my parents were married and to each other."

"You're enjoying this."

His smile belied his words. "It's purely business, I assure you. But I appreciate you considering sleeping with me."

She fought the urge to slap his handsome face. "I never—"

"I'm sure you have never," he said. "But we can deal with that later. Right now, I suggest we discuss this over breakfast. I'm starved." He moved away, finally giving her breathing room. "You're buying."

"I don't think so." She was trembling inside, her stomach doing slow somersaults. The man threw her off balance, and he knew it. That made it even worse. She took a couple of deep breaths, shocked that some reporter could get this kind of primitive response from her.

Finally she turned to face him. He was going through her photos with an apparent critical eye. She wanted to grab them from him. The last thing she needed was a critique from him about her art.

"Call the police." She crossed her arms over her chest. "If you think you can blackmail me—"

"These are good, really," he said, turning to look at her as if surprised. "You have a good eye."

She hated how pleased she was, but quickly mentally shook herself. What did he know about photography anyway? Just because he carried around a camera and took underhanded snapshots of people who didn't want their photos taken...

"I'd hoped we could discuss this over pancakes," he said as he stepped away from her photos. "I know something about your mother that you're going to want to hear before you see it in the media."

"There is nothing you can tell me that I would—"

"Your mother isn't just lying about the past twenty-two years. She's been lying since the get-go, and I can prove it." He smiled. "But first I want breakfast. I'm starved."

Don't miss LUCKY SHOT by B.J. Daniels
available wherever HQN books and ebooks are sold.